A GIRL OF THE PEOPLE

L. T. Meade

1st WORLD
LIBRARY
Literary Society

A Girl of the People

L. T. Meade

© 1st World Library – Literary Society, 2004
PO Box 2211
Fairfield, IA 52556
www.1stworldlibrary.org
First Edition

LCCN: 2004195335

Softcover ISBN: 1-4218-0166-3
Hardcover ISBN: 1-4218-0066-7
eBook ISBN: 1-4218-0266-X

Purchase *"A Girl of the People"*
as a traditional bound book at:
www.1stWorldLibrary.org/purchase.asp?ISBN=1-4218-0166-3

1st World Library Literary Society is a nonprofit
organization dedicated to promoting literacy by:

- Creating a free internet library accessible from any
computer worldwide.
- Hosting writing competitions and offering book
publishing scholarships.

A Girl of the People
contributed by Tim, Ed & Rodney
in support of
1st World Library Literary Society

CHAPTER I.

"You have kept us waiting an age! Come along, Bet, do."

"She ain't going to funk it, surely!"

"No, no, not she, - she's a good 'un, Bet is, - come along, Bet. Joe Wilkins is waiting for us round the corner, and he says Sam is to be there, and Jimmy, and Hester Wright: do come along, now."

"Will Hester Wright sing?" suddenly demanded the girl who was being assailed by all these remarks.

"Yes, tip-top, a new song from one of the music halls in London. Now then, be you coming or not, Bet?"

"No, no, she's funking it," suddenly called out a dancing little sprite of a newspaper girl. She came up close to Bet as she spoke, and shook a dirty hand in her face, and gazed up at her with two mirthful, teasing, wicked black eyes. "Bet's funking it, - she's a mammy's girl, - she's tied to her mammy's apron-strings, he-he-he!"

The other girls all joined in the laugh; and Bet, who was standing stolid and straight in the centre of the group, first flushed angrily , then turned pale and bit her lips.

"I ain't funking," she said; "nobody can ever say as there's any funk about me, - there's my share. Good-night."

She tossed a shilling on to the pavement, and before the astonished girls could intercept her, turned on her heel and marched away.

A mocking laugh or two floated after her on the night air, then the black-eyed girl picked up the shilling, said Bet was a "good 'un, though she wor that contrairy," and the whole party set off singing and shouting, up the narrow street of this particular Liverpool slum.

Bet, when she left her companions, walked quickly in the direction of the docks; the pallor still continued on her brown cheeks, and a dazed expression filled her heavy eyes.

"They clinched it when they said I wor a mammy's girl," she muttered. "There ain't no funk in me, but there was a look about mother this morning that I couldn't a-bear. No, I ain't a mammy's girl, not I. There was never nought so good about me, and I have give away my last shilling, - flung it into the gutter. Well, never mind. I ain't tied to nobody's apron-strings - no, not I. Wish I wor, wish I wor."

She walked on, not too fast, holding herself very stiff and erect now. She was a tall girl, made on a large and generous scale, her head was well set on a pair of shapely shoulders, and her coils of red-brown hair were twisted tightly round her massive head.

L. T. Meade

"Bet," said a young lad, as he rushed up the street - "ha-ha, handsome Bet, give us a kiss, will ye?"

Bet rewarded him with a smart cuff across his face, and marched on, more defiant than ever.

As she paused at a certain door a sweet-looking girl with a white face, dressed in the garb of a Sister, came out.

"Ah, Elizabeth, I am glad you have arrived," she said. "I have just left your mother; she has been crying for you, and - and - she is very ill indeed."

"Oh, I know that, Sister Mary; let me go upstairs now."

Bet pushed past the girl almost rudely, and ascended the dark rickety stairs with a light step. Her head was held very far back, and in her eyes there was a curious mixture of defiance, softness and despair. Two little boys, with the same reddish-brown hair as hers, were playing noisily on the fourth landing. They made a rush at Bet when they saw her, climbed up her like little cats, and half strangled her with their thin half-naked arms.

"Bet, Bet, I say, mother's awful bad. Bet, speak to Nat; he stole my marble, he did. Fie on you, Cap'n; you shouldn't have done it."

"I like that!" shouted the ragged boy addressed as "Cap'n." "You took it from me first, you know you did, Gen'ral."

"If mother's bad, you shouldn't make a noise," said Bet, flinging the two little boys away, with no particular gentleness. "There, of course I'll kiss you, Gen'ral - poor little lad. Go down now and play on the next landing, and keep quiet for the next ten minutes if it's in you."

"Bet," whispered the youngest boy, who was known as "Cap'n," "shall I tell yer what mother did this morning?"

"No, no; I don't want to hear - go downstairs and keep quiet, *do.*"

"Oh, yer'll be in such a steaming rage! She burnt yer book, yer *Jane Eyre* as yer wor reading - lor, it were fine - the bit as you read to the Gen'ral and me, but she said as it wor a hell-fire book, and she burnt it - I seed her, and so did the Gen'ral - she pushed it between the bars with the poker. She got up in her night-things to do it, and then she got back to bed again, and she panted for nearly an hour after - didn't she, Gen'ral?"

"Yes - yes - come along, come along. Look at Bet! she's going to strike some 'un - look at her; didn't we say as she'd be in a steaming rage. Come, Cap'n."

The little boys scuttled downstairs, shouting and tumbling over one another in their flight. Bet stood perfectly still on the landing. The boys were right when they said she would be in a rage; her heart beat heavily, her face was white, and for an instant she pressed her forehead against the door of her mother's room and clenched her teeth.

The book burnt! the poor book which had given her pleasure, and which she had saved up her pence to buy - the book which had drawn her out of herself, and made her forget her wretched surroundings, committed to the flames - ignominiously destroyed, and called bad names, too. How dared her mother do it? how dared she? The girls were right when they said she was tied to apron-strings - she was, she was! But she would bear it no longer. She would show her mother that she would submit to no leading - that she, Elizabeth Granger, the handsomest newspaper girl in Liverpool, was a woman, and her own mistress.

"She oughtn't to have done it," half-groaned Bet "The poor book! And I'll never know now what's come to Jane and Rochester - I'll never know. It cuts me to the quick. Mother oughtn't to take pleasure from one like that, but it's all of a piece. Well, I'll go in and say 'good night' to her, and then I'll go back to the girls. I'm sorry I've lost my evening's spree, but I can hear Hester Wright sing, leastways; and mebbe she'll let me walk home with her."

With one hand Bet brushed something like moisture from her eyes; with the other she opened the door of her mother's room, and went in. Her entrance was noisy, and as she stood on the threshold her expression was defiant. Then all in a second the girl's face changed; a soft, troubled, hungry look filled her eyes; she glided forward without even making the boards creak. In Bet's absence the room had undergone a transformation. A bright fire burned in a carefully polished grate; in front of the hearth a thick knitted rug was placed; the floor was tidy, the two or three rickety chairs were in order, the wooden mantel-piece was free of dust. Over her mother's bed a soft crimson counterpane was thrown, and her mother, half sitting up, rested her white face against the snowy pillows. A little table stood near the bedside, which contained some cordial in a glass. The sick woman's long thin hands lay outside the crimson counterpane, and her eyes, dark and wistful, were turned in the direction of the door. Bet went straight up to the bed: the transformation in the room was nothing to her; she saw it, and guessed quickly that Sister Mary had done it; but the look, the changed look on her mother's face, was everything. She forgot her own wrongs and the burnt book; her heart was filled with a wild fear, a dreary sense of coming desolation seized her, and clasping her mother's long thin fingers in her own brown strong hands, she bent down and whispered in a husky voice,

"Mother - oh, mother!"

The woman looked up and smiled.

"You've come back, Bet?" she said. "Give me a drop of the cordial. I'm glad you've come back. I thought it might have been the will of Him who knows best that I should die without seeing of you again, Elizabeth."

"Oh, no, mother - of course I've come back. I hurried home. I didn't stay for nobody. How nice the room looks, mother - and the kettle boils. I'll make you a cup o' tea."

"No, Bet, I don't want it; stoop down, and look at me. Bet, look me in the eyes - oh, my girl, my girl!"

Bet gazed unflinchingly at her mother. The two faces were somewhat alike - the same red gleam in the brown eyes, the same touch of red on the abundant hair; but one face was tired, worn out, and the other was fresh and full and plump. Both faces had certain lines of hardness, certain indications of stormy,

L. T. Meade

troublous souls looking through the eyes, and speaking on the lips.

"I'm going to die, Bet; Fin going back to the good God," panted Mrs. Granger." he doctor have been, and he says mebbe it'll last till morning, mebbe not. I'm going back to Him as knows best, - it's a rare sight of good fortune for me, ain't it?"

"I don't believe you're going to die," said Bet. She spoke harshly, in an effort to subdue the emotion which was making her tremble all over. "Doctors are allays a-frightening folks. Have a cup o' tea, mother?"

"It don't frighten me, Bet," said Mrs. Granger. "I'm going away, and He's coming to fetch me; I ain't afeard. I never seemed more of a poor sort of a body than I do to-night, but somehow I ain't afeard. When He comes He'll be good - I know He'll be good to me."

"Oh, you're ready fast enough, mother," said Bet, with some bitterness. "No one has less call to talk humble than you, mother. You was allays all for good, as you calls it."

"I was reg'lar at church, and I did my dooty," answered Mrs. Granger. "But somehow I feels poor and humble to-night. Mebbe I didn't go the right way to make you think well on religion, Bet. Mebbe I didn't do nothing right - only I tried, I tried."

There was a piteous note in the voice, and a quivering of the thin austere lips, which came to Bet as a revelation. Her own trembling increased violently; she threw herself down by the bedside and sobs shook her.

"Mother, mother, it have all been hateful, hateful," she moaned. "And oh, mother, why did you burn my book?"

There was no answer. The white thin hand rested with a certain tremble on the girl's thick hair.

"Why did you burn my book, that gave me pleasure, mother?" said Bet, raising her head, and speaking with her old defiance.

"I thought," began Mrs. Granger, - "mebbe I did wrong, - mebbe I were too 'ard. Him that knows best will forgive me."

"Oh, mother, mother! I forgive you from the bottom of my heart."

Bet took one of the thin hands, and covered it with passionate kisses.

"I ain't good," she said, "and I don't want to die. It floors me, mother, how you can be glad to go down into the grave and stay there - ugh!"

"I ain't going to stay there," replied the dying woman, in a faint though confident voice.

She was silent then for a few moments, but there was a shining, satisfied light in her eyes; and her lips opened once or twice, as if to speak. Bet held one of her hands firmly, and her own eager hungry eyes never stirred from the dying, tired-out face.

"Bet."

"Yes, mother."

"You'll make me a bit of promise afore I go?"

"A promise, mother?"

"Yes, a promise. Oh, Bet, a promise from you means an awful lot. You don't break your word. You're as strong as strong, - and if you promise me this, you'll be splendid - you'll be - give me a drop of the cordial, child, - you'll be - I have been praying about it all day, I have been saying, 'Lord, send Bet in gentle-like, and trackable-like, and with no anger nourished in her heart, and, and, - another sip, child - the breath's short - I - you'll make me the promise, won't you, child?"

"Oh yes, poor mother, if I can!"

"Yes, you can; and it'll be so splendid. There, I'm stronger, now. Him as knows has given me the strength. Why, you're me over again, Bet, but you're twice as grand as me. You're me without my frets, and my contrariness. Fancy, Bet, what you'd be in this 'ere place ef you made that promise. Why, strong? - strong 'ud be no word for it! You, with never your temper let out like a raging lion! There'd be no one as could stand agen you, Bet. Your father, - why your father 'd give up the bad ways and the drink. And the little boys, - the little boys, - oh, Bet, Bet, ef you'd only make the promise it 'ud save them all from hell-fire."

"I'll do what I can mother. See, you're wasting all your poor breath. I'll do what I can. You say it all out, and don't tremble so, poor mother."

"Hold my hands, then, child; look me in the face, say

the words after me - oh, my poor breath, my poor breath - God give me strength just to say the words. Bet, you hear. Bet, say them after me - 'From this moment out I promise to take up with religion, so help me, Lord God Almighty!'"

The woman said the words eagerly, with sudden and intense fire and passion; her whole soul was in them - her dying hands hurt the girl with the firmness of their grip.

"Bet, Bet - you hain't spoke - you hain't spoke!"

"No, no, mother - I can't - not them words - no, mother."

Bet sat down again by the side of the bed; her face was buried in the crimson counterpane; a dry moan or two escaped her lips.

"I'd do anything for mother - anything now as she's really going away, but I couldn't take up with religion," she sobbed. "Oh, it's a mistake - all a mistake, and it ain't meant for one like me. Why, *I*, if I were religious - why, I'd have to turn into a hypocrite - why, - I - I'd scorn myself. Yes, mother, what are you saying? Yes, mother, I'd do anything to make your death-bed easy - anything but this."

Bet had fancied she had heard her mother speaking; the perfect stillness now alarmed her far more than any words, and she lifted her head with a start. Mrs. Granger was lying motionless, but she was neither dead nor had she fainted. Her restless hands were quiet, and her worn-out face, although it looked deadly pale, was peaceful. Here eyes looked a little upwards, and in them there was a contented smile. Bet saw the look, and nothing in all the world could have horrified her more. Her mother, who thought religion beyond anything else, had just heard her say that never, never, even to smooth a dying pillow, could she, Bet, take up with the ways of the religious; and yet her eyes smiled and she looked content.

"Mother, you don't even care," said Bet, in an anguish of pain and inconsistency.

"O, yes, child, I care; but I seem to hear Him as knows best saying 'Leave it to me.' I ain't fretting, child; I has come to a place where no one frets, and you're either all in despair, or you're as still and calm and happy" - here she broke off abruptly. "Bet, I want yer to be good to the little boys - to stand atween them and their father, and not to larn them no bad ways They're wild little chaps, and they take to the bad as easy as easy; but you can do whatever yer likes with them. Your father, he don't care for nobody, and he'd do them an ill turn; but you'll stand atween them and him - d'ye hear, Bet?"

"Yes, mother - I'll make a promise about that, if you like."

"No, no; you never broke your word, and saying it once'll content me."

"Mother," said Bet, suddenly. "Mebbe you'd like the little chaps to turn religious. As you've allays set such a deal of store on prayers and sich like, mebbe you'd like it for them?"

"Oh, yes, Bet - oh, my poor gel, has the Lord seen fit

to soften yer hard heart?"

"Look here, mother," - here the tall, splendidly-made girl stood up, and throwing back her head, and with the firelight full on her face, and reflecting a new, strange expression of excitement, she spoke suddenly: "I can't promise the other, but I'll promise this. The little boys' lives shall come afore my life - harm shall come to me afore it touches them; and ef religion can do anything for them, why, they shall hear of it and choose for themselves. There, I have promised."

CHAPTER II.

MRS. Granger lingered all through that night, but she scarcely said anything more, and in the cold dawn of the morning her spirit passed very quietly away. The two little boys opened the room door noisily at midnight, but they too were impressed, as Bet had been, by the unusual order and appearance of comfort of the room. Perhaps they were also startled by the girl's still figure crouching by the bedside, and by the look on their mother's face as she lay with her eyes closed, breathing hard and fast. They ceased to talk noisily, and crept over to a straw mattress on the floor which they shared together. When they next opened their eyes they were motherless.

Mrs. Granger died between five and six in the morning; and when the breath had quite left her body Bet arose, stretched herself, - for she was quite stiff from sitting so long in one position, - and going downstairs, woke a neighbor who occupied a room on the next floor.

"Mrs. Bennett, my mother is dead; can you take care of the Cap'n and the Gen'ral this morning? I'll pay you for it when I sell my papers to-night."

Mrs. Bennett was a wrinkled old woman of about sixty-five. She was deeply interested in tales of death and calamity, and instantly offered not only to do what she could for the boys, but to go upstairs and assist in the laying out of the dead woman.

"No, no; I'll do what's wanted myself," replied Bet; "ef you'll take the boys I'll bring them down asleep as they are, and I'll be ever so much obligated. No, don't come upstairs, please. Father'll be in presently, and then him and me and mother must be alone; for I've a word to say to father, and no one must hear me."

Bet went back to the room where her mother had died. She was very tired, and her limbs were stiff and ached badly after the long night's vigil she had gone through. No particular or overwhelming grief oppressed her. On the whole, she had loved her mother better than any other human being; but the time for grief, and the awful sense of not having her to turn to, had not yet arrived; she was only conscious of a very solemn promise made, and of an overpowering sense of weariness. She lay down on the bed beside the dead woman, and fell into a sound and dreamless slumber.

In about an hour's time noisy steps were heard ascending the stairs. The littleboys, cuddling close to one another in Mrs. Bennett's bed, heard them, and clasped each other's hands in alarm; but Bet sound, very sound, asleep did not know when her father reeled into the room. He had been out all night - a common practice of his - and he ought to have been fairly sober now, for the public-houses had been shut for many hours, but a boon companion had taken him home for a private carouse. He was more tipsy than he had ever been known to be at that hour of the morning, and consequently more savage. He entered the room where his dead wife and his young daughter lay, cursing and

L. T. Meade

muttering, - a bad man every inch of him - terrible just then in his savage imbecility.

"Bet," he said, "Bet, get up. Martha, I want my cup of tea. Get it for me at once - I say, at once! I'm an hour late now for the docks, and Jim Targent will get my job. I must have my tea, - my head's reeling! Get up, Martha, or I'll kick you!"

"I'll get you the tea, father," said Bet.

She had risen instantly at the sound of his voice. "Set down in that chair and keep still; keep still, I say - you'd better."

She pushed him on to a hard wooden chair, shaking him not a little as she did so.

"There, I'll put the kettle on and make the tea for you - not that I'll ever do it again - no, never, as long as I live. There, you'd better set quiet, or not one drop shall pass your lips."

"Why don't the woman get it for me?" growled Granger. "I didn't mean you to be awoke, Bet. Young gels must have their slumber out. Why don't the woman see to her duty?"

"She has done her duty, father. You set still, and you shall have the tea presently."

The man glared at his daughter with his bloodshot eyes. She had been up all night, and her hair was tossed, and her eyes smarted; but beside him she looked so fresh, so upright, so brave and strong, that he himself in some undefinable way felt the contrast, and shrank from her. He turned his uneasy gaze towards the bed; he would vent his spite on that weak wife of his - Martha should know what it was to keep a man with a splitting headache waiting for his tea. He made an effort to rise, and to approach the bed, but Bet forestalled him.

"Set you there, or you'll drink no tea in this house," she said; and then, taking a shawl, she threw it over an old clothes-screen, and placed it between Granger and his dead wife.

The kettle boiled at last, the tea was made strong ang good, and Bet took a cup to her father. He drained it off at one long draught, and held out his shaking hand to have the cup refilled. Bet supplied him with a second draught, then she placed her hand with the air of a professional nurse on his wrist.

"You're better now, father."

"That I am, gel, and thank you. You're by no means a bad sort, Bet - worth twenty of her, I can tell you."

"Leave her out of the question, if you please, father, or you'll get no help from me. You'd like to wash your face, mebbe?"

"Yes, yes, with cold water. Give me your hand, child, and I'll get up."

"Set you still - I'll fetch the water."

She brought it in a tin pail, with a piece of flannel and soap and a coarse towel.

L. T. Meade

"Now, wash - wash and make yourself as clean as you can - for you has got to see summut - leastways you can take the outside dirt away; there, make yourself clean while I lets the daylight in."

The man washed and laved himself. He was becoming gradually sober, and Bet's words had a subduing effect; he looked after her with a certain maudlin admiration, as she drew up the blind, and let the uncertain daylight into the poor little room. Then she went behind the screen, and he heard her for a moment or two moving about. He dried his face and hands and hair and was standing up, looking comparatively fresh and another man, when she returned to him.

"You're not a bad sort of a gel," he said, attempting to chuck her under the chin, only she drew away from him. "You know what a man wants, and you get it for him and don't hurl no ugly words in his face. Well, I'm off to the docks now. I'll let the old 'ooman sleep on, this once, and tell her what I think on her, and how much more I set store by that daughter of hers, tonight."

"You'll let her sleep on, will you?" said Bet.

Her tone was queer and constrained; even her father noticed it.

"She is asleep now; come and look at her; you may wake her if you can."

"No, no, gel; let me get off - Jim Targent will get my berth unless I look sharp. Let me be, Bet - your mother can sleep her fill this morning,"

"Come and look at her, father; come - you must."

She took his hand - she was very strong - stronger than him at that moment, for his legs were not steady, and even now he was scarcely sober.

"I don't want to see an old 'ooman asleep," he muttered, but he let the strong hand lead him forward. Bet pushed back the screen, and drew him close to the bed.

"Wake her if you can," she said, and her eyes blazed into his.

Granger looked. There was no mistaking what he saw.

"My God!" he murmured. "Bet, you shouldn't have done it - you shouldn't have broke it to me like this!"

He trembled all over.

"Martha dead! Let me get away. I *hate* dead people."

"Put your hand on her forehead, father. See, she couldn't have got your tea for you. It were no fault of her'n - you beat her, and you kicked her, and you made life awful for her; but you couldn't hurt her this morning; she's above you now, you can't touch her now."

"Let me go, Bet - you're an awful girl - you had no call to give me a turn like this. No, I won't touch her, and you can't force me. I'm going out - I won't stay in this room. I'm going down to the docks - I mustn't lose my work. What do you say - that I shan't go? Where will you all be if I don't arn your bread for you?"

"Set down there on the side of the bed, father. I'll keep you five minutes and no more. You needn't be all in a tremble - you needn't be showing of the white feather. Bless you, she never could hurt you less than she does now. Set there, and look at her face. I've a word or two to say, and I can only say it with you looking at her dead face. Then you can go down to the docks, and stay there for always as far as it matters to me."

She pushed the man on to the bed. He could see the white, still face of his dead wife. The tired look had left it; the wrinkles had almost disappeared. Martha Granger looked twenty years younger than she had done yesterday.

Around the closed eyelids, around the softly smiling mouth, lay an awful peace and grandeur. The drunken husband looked at the wife whom he had abused, whose days he had rendered one long misery, and a lump arose in his throat; a queer new sensation, which he could not recognize as either remorse or repentance, filled his breast. He no longer opposed Bet; he gazed fixedly, with a stricken stare, at the dead woman.

"Speak, gel; say what you have to say," he muttered.

"It's only a word or two, father - It's just this. Mother's dead, and in a day or two she'll be buried. You worn't there to bid her good-bye, and it ain't likely you'll ever meet her again, unless that's true about the Judgment Day. Maybe it is true, and maybe mother will tell God some ugly things about you then, father. Maybe you'll see her then for a minute or two - I can't say."

"Don't," said Granger. "You're awful when you likes, Bet. You has me down, and you tramples on me.

You're a cruel gel, and no mistake."

A derisive smile came to Bet's face.

"Mother's dead and she'll be buried," she continued, in a dry, monotonous voice. "The money is in the burying club for her, and she can be laid in the grave decent like. Then me and the boys, Nat and Thady, we're going away. I wanted to say that - I wanted to say that your ways aren't our ways, and so we'd best part company; and I wanted to say here, with you looking at mother's dead face, and her smiling back at you so awful and still, and the good God, if there is a God, listening, that I has promised mother that the boys Nat and Thady - the Cap'n and Gen'ral, as they're called here - shan't larn your ways, which are bad past belief; so when mother's buried, we're going away. That's all. You can go to the docks, now."

As Bet spoke she took a little white soft handkerchief, and laid it gently over her mother's face.

"You can go now," she repeated, and she opened the door for the man, who slunk out of the room. He was half-sober, half-stupefied. A burning rage, which was neither remorse nor repentance, and yet was a mixture of both, surged up in his heart. He said to himself, that he was sorry for Martha, who was dead, and quite beyond his reach any more; but he hated Bet, for she had humbled him and dared to defy him.

CHAPTER III.

In Liverpool there are, perhaps more than in any town in the world, all sorts and conditions of men. The very wealthy and the very poor are to be found within its precincts - also the very good and the very bad. Its slums are black and awful; but it also contains some of the finest public buildings, some of the most massive and comfortable houses, and without any exception the largest and greatest docks, in the world. All nationalities come to Liverpool. It sees life from beyond the seas, it has a population of people always coming and going - Americans who go to the theatre in London and arrive in Liverpool about three in the morning, on their return to their own country; Irishmen, Scotchmen, dwellers in Africa; in fact, people from all parts of the civilized world find their way to Liverpool, to return from thence by way of the sea to their native lands. On certain days in the week the hotels and lodging-houses are packed to overflowing; the different piers present scenes of activity and bustle; the great ships come and go, and the people come and go with them - Liverpool is passed through and forgotten.

That is the case with those fleeting crowds who so largely contribute to its trade and prosperity; but the *habitue'* of Liverpool, the man who spends his days there, is a totally different order of being. The stranger sees the great city most generally through mist and fog;

he regards the pavements as rough and slippery; he thinks the public buildings large, but ugly. Liverpool to him is another London, but without London's attractions. But the true Liverpool man looks at his native town from a very different point of view. He is part and parcel of the place, and he loves it for its size and ugliness, its great commerce, its thriving active business life. Liverpool to its citizens means home; they are proud of their laws and their customs; they like to dispense charity in their own way; they like to support and help their own poor; they have, to an extent absolutely unknown in London, the true spirit of neighborliness. This spirit is shared by all alike, the rich and the poor feel it, and it binds them together; they regard their town as the world, and look askance at inventions and ideas imported from other places. There are bad slums in Liverpool, and wicked deeds committed, and cruel rough men to be found in multitudes; but the evil there compared to London seems at least to be conquerable - the slums can be got at; nobody who chooses to apply in the right quarter need die of famine or distress.

Most of the men are dock-laborers; they are often taken on only for half a day at a time, and in this way their work is precarious, and, except for the most steady-going and respectable, at many periods of the year very hard to get. Almost all the men either work at the docks, or take to a sea-faring life. Thus sailors are coming and going, and there is scarcely a family belonging either to high or low who has not a son, a brother, or a father on the sea. Perhaps this is one of the facts which binds the people to one another - the rich lady in her carriage, and the poor starved, gaunt woman who lives in one room up many pairs of stairs in a dismal back slum, look alike out on the waters of the Mersey for the boy who may come back any day with the taste of the sea about him.

The Liverpool boy has his work cut out for him; those who wish to belong emphatically to the place of their birth, either earn what they can at the docks or go to sea. They need never debate as to their profession or their calling in life; it is cut out for them - it lies at their feet with that sea which is brought by the ships to their very doors.

But the Liverpool girl - that is, the girl of the people - is not so fortunate. She has no special work provided for her; she is not like the Manchester girl, who is as certain to go into the factory as she is to eat and drink - there are scarcely any factories in Liverpool, and a very tiny proportion of girls find work there.

Domestic service is hated by the Liverpool lass. At one time, when forced by necessity to adopt this means of earning her bread, she made a stipulation that she should at least sleep at home - that her evenings from seven o'clock out should be her own. Now that this rule is no longer allowed, domestic service is held in less esteem than ever, and only the most sensible girls dream of availing themselves of its comforts.

While the boys, therefore, are earning and striking out independent paths for themselves, the girls are under difficulties. They must earn money; for life is not too easy to live in their native place, and each must bring in his or her small portion of help to the family purse; but how, is the difficulty. Some hawk fruit and vegetables, doing a fairly brisk trade on Saturdays, and even on Sunday mornings; but the most favored Liverpool girls earn their daily bread by selling newspapers night after night in the streets. A good-looking girl will secure her regular customers, have her own regular and undisturbed beat, and will often earn from tenpence to a shilling a night; but the newspaper beats have to be bought, and often at a high figure, for competition is very keen, and the coveted corners where the greater number of gentlemen are to be met that require evening papers are highly prized.

Bet Granger had been a newspaper girl for a couple of years now; her mother had saved up money to buy her beat for her; it was one of the best in the town, and she was always so trim and neat, so comely and pleasant-looking, and her papers so clean and crisp and neatly cut, that she did a fair trade, and largely helped to support her mother and little brothers. Her trade occupied her for a couple of hours every evening. In the morning, as the mood took her, she helped her mother with plain needlework - Mrs. Granger worked for a wholesale shop at the usual shop prices - or she went down to the docks.

Every Liverpool girl is fond of watching the ships as they come in or go out; they connect her with the outer life, with the far-away world - they give her a pleasing and ever-recurring sense of excitement and exhila-ration; but, as a rule, they never implant in her breast that fever to be off and away which so soon affects the Liverpool boy.

Bet liked to watch the ships. She would stand erect and almost haughty in her bearing, often quite close to the edge of the quays, speaking very few words, and making scarcely any acquaintances, but thinking many strange and undefined thoughts in her untutored heart.

L. T. Meade

The Grangers did not belong to the lowest of the people. Granger was a clever workman. He was seldom out of employment; for although he drank away his earnings, and gave no thought whatever to the comfort of his wife and children, he was sober and steady by day. He had a clever, shrewd head, as yet unaffected by drink, and he did the work allotted to him in a superior manner to most of his class.

When first they were married, he and his wife had two bright, cheery rooms. They were well furnished, and things promised brightly for the couple. Granger, however, was the son of a drunkard, and the sins of the father were soon to be abundantly visited on him. Mrs. Granger meant well, but her religion was not of an inspiriting kind. Whenever she saw her husband the worse for drink she reproached him, and spoke to him about hell-fire. He soon ceased to care for her; and even when Bet was a tiny child she scarcely ever remembered an evening which did not find her mother in tears, and her father returning home, having taken a great deal more than was good for him.

Years went by; children were born, only to live for a day or two and to pass away. Mrs. Granger became more broken-down and unhappy-looking every year, and Bet grew into a tall, comely girl. She was not particularly gentle, nor particularly amiable, and she had the worst possible training for such a nature as hers; but nevertheless she had a certain nobility about her. For instance, no one had ever heard Elizabeth Granger tell a lie. She was proud of her truthfulness, which was simply the result of courage. She was afraid of no one, and no circumstance had ever caused her cheek to blanch with fear. She quickly acquired a name for truth and honesty of purpose, and then pride helped her to live up to her character. She was not very quick to give promises, but she often boasted that, once she gave one, nothing would ever induce her to break it. She was very fiery and hot-tempered, but as a rule she did not fly out about trifles, and there was a certain grandeur about her nature which accorded well with her fine physique and upright bearing.

Bet was an only child for several years. It is true that many little brothers and sisters had been carried away to the cemetery, but none lived until two puny boys put in so feeble an appearance that the neighbors thought the miserable thing called life could not exist in their tiny persons more than a day or two. They were twins, and Mrs. Granger nearly died when she gave them birth. The neighbors said that it would be a good thing if the broken-down mother and the babes that nobody wanted all went away together.

"There's a deal too many children in the world," they said; "it would be good if they was took, poor lambs."

But here Bet, who overheard the words, gave way to one of her bursts of fury. She turned the offending but well-disposed neighbors out of the room; she locked the door, and kneeling down by the babies, gave them a perfect baptism of tears and kisses.

"Who says as they're not wanted?" she sobbed. "I want 'em - I'm allays a-wanting something, and maybe they'll fill my heart."

From this moment she constituted herself the babies' devoted nurse; and so, after a fashion, they throve, and did not die.

The darker the times grew for Mrs. Granger the more she clung to her religion. She had a real belief, a real although dim faith. The belief supported her tottering steps, and the faith kept her worn spirit from utterly fainting; but they did nothing to illumine or render happy the lives of those about her. She believed intensely in a God who punished. He saved - she knew He saved - but only through fire. In the dark winter evenings she poured out her stern thoughts, her unlovely ideas, into the ears of her young daughter. As a child Bet listened in terror; as a woman she simply ceased to believe.

"Ef God were like that, she'd have nought to do with Him," - this was her thought of thoughts. She refused to accompany her mother to chapel on Sundays; she left the room when the Bible was read aloud; she made one or two friends for herself, and these friends were certainly not of her mother's choosing. She could read, and she loved novels - indeed, she would devour books of any kind, but she had to hide them from her mother, who thought it her duty, as she valued her daughter's immortal soul, to commit them to the flames.

The mother loved the girl, and never ceased to wrestle in prayer for her, and to believe she would shine as a jewel in her crown some day; and the girl also cared for the mother, respecting her stern sense of duty, admiring the length of her prayers, wondering at her ceaseless devotion; but both were outwardly hard to the other, showing no softness, and speaking of no love.

All Bet's up-bringing was hardening; and but for the presence of the boys she might have wondered if she possessed any heart at all.

She was nineteen when her mother suddenly broke down completely in health, and after the shortest of illnesses - too short to alarm anyone, too short for even the word danger to be whispered - closed her eyes on this world, leaving Bet in a state of bewildered and impotent rage.

There was no longer the faintest doubt in her orphaned heart that she loved her mother.

CHAPTER IV.

Bet wept silently for the greater part of the day which saw her motherless, but in the evening she went out as usual to sell her papers. Her eyes were swollen from the heavy and constant tears she shed, but she had neatly plaited her hair and wound it round her comely head, and she carried herself with even a little more defiance than usual. She was miserable to-night, and she felt that the whole world was against her.

The night, for the time of year was November, was quite in accordance with her feelings. It was damp, a drizzling mist was blown into her face, and the pavements were slippery with that peculiar Liverpool mud which exceeds even London mud in slipperiness. Bet's beat, however, was brightly lighted; there was a public-house at one corner, and a little further up were two gentlemen's clubs. All were brilliant with gaslight, and the girl, wrapping her shawl about her - she wore no hat or bonnet - took her accustomed stand. She always avoided the public-house - not because she feared its tipsy inhabitants, but because she knew no sale for her wares lay there. Her favorite stand was under a lamp post, close to the largest of the clubs. The light of the lamp fell full on her face and figure, and shone on the evening papers which she offered for sale. Her customers came up as usual, bought what they required of her, one or two giving her a careless and some a friendly "good-evening." No one noticed her pallid cheeks, nor the heavy depths of trouble in her red-brown eyes. Her luck, however, was good, and she had almost sold all her little stock of papers, when a vibrating and rather peculiar voice at her elbow caused her to start and turn quickly.

"Is that you, Hester Wright?" she said, speaking in an almost pettish voice. "Well, I can't go with you to-night, no how; I'm off home this minute."

"Why, Bet, is yer mother took worse?" asked the voice. It vibrated again, and two sweet though rather wild-looking eyes gazed full into Bet's tired, white face.

"Mother," said the girl. She made a valiant struggle, but no more words would come.

After about a moment she spoke in a strained and totally altered voice:

"Let me be for to-night, Hester. I've sold my papers, and I'm going home."

"No, you're not, honey; you're coming along o' me. Don't I see as yer white with the grief, and half distraught like. There, I'm alone tonight, unless Will should drop in; come and have a cup o' tea with me, Bet."

"My mother's dead, Hester," said Bet. She could speak without effort now, but the tears were raining down her cheeks.

"Poor lamb! Dead? Well, I thought as the blow would come. You come home with me, Elizabeth. Maybe I'll sing something to you."

At this proposition Bet changed color.

"I'm starved for that voice of yours, Hester," she said. And then she put her hand through her companion's arm, and they walked off at a quiet pace together. Hester was as tall as Bet, and about ten years her senior. She was very slender, and carried herself well; her eyes were dark and beautiful, otherwise she had a queer, irregularly formed face. Her jet-black hair grew low on her forehead, and when she smiled, which she only did occasionally, she showed the gleam of very white teeth. No one called Hester Wright handsome, but few women of her class in Liverpool had a wider influence. She had a peculiar voice, rather deep set, and, at least in speaking, only admitting of a limited range of compass; but every word spoken by her was so nicely adjusted, so carefully modulated, that the simplest and most ill-formed sentence acquired a rude eloquence. This was her speaking voice. When she sang, it rose into power; it was then a deep contralto, utterly untaught, but free and easy as the notes of a bird. Hester could do what she liked with men and women when she sang to them, and she knew her power. In her own circle she was more or less of a queen, and although she was no better and no richer than the poorest of the Liverpool girls, yet her smallest word of approbation was treasured almost as if it had been a royal gift. She had a great insight into character; she had large tact, and she was also affectionate.

Bet in her heart of hearts had a boundless admiration for this woman, and she felt a sense of comfort stealing over her as they walked quickly through the wet, slippery streets side by side.

Hester lived in a little room, which she managed to keep fairly neat and clean, quite close to the docks. In the daytime you could see the masts of the tall ships from her window, and the language of the sailors and the many shouts of the workers on the quays could be borne into her room on the breeze. Now the window was curtained, and a little fire shed a cheerful reflection on the dingy walls. Hester stirred the fire, threw on an additional lump or two of coal, and drawing a three-legged stool forward for Bet, motioned to her to seat herself. The room was fairly warm, and Bet was glad to dry her damp dress, and to spread out her hands before the cheerful blaze. As Hester bustled about, and laid a tiny table with plates for three, she gradually drew from Bet a little of the story of last night.

"I have promised," said Bet, in conclusion, "to keep the two littl'uns safe - that's my work now, and I told father this morning what he wor to expect."

"And how did he take it, honey?" said Hester. "He knew you, Bet. He knew as you weren't a girl to say one thing and mean another."

"Yes, he knew that," answered Bet. "Most folks know that of me," she continued, with a heavy sigh.

"Well, have some tea now, honey - draw up to the table. The butter's good, and the red-herring done to a turn. I expected Will Scarlett in, but we won't wait for him. Ah! here he is - just in the nick o' time."

The door was opened, and a young sailor, with a certain resemblance to Hester both in face and figure, stepped across the threshold. He colored up under his brown skin when he saw Bet, but she scarcely noticed him, and gave him her hand in limp fashion, her eyes hardly raised.

"My ship sails to-morrow, Hester," he said, "the 'Good Queen Anne,' - I've got a rattling good berth this time, and no mistake."

He tossed off his cap as he spoke, again glanced at Bet with a certain shyness, and then dropped into the seat opposite to her.

"Help yourself, Will," said Hester. "Bet's in a bit o' trouble - you mustn't mind her; she wor telling me things, and she'll have a hard fight afore her, I can see. Well, I say she must keep up heart. Have some tea, honey? Will, don't you make two mouths of a cherry - put the whole of that herring on your plate - there are more in the bag for me to toast when this is finished."

"I can't eat, Hester - it's no use," said Bet.

She rose from the table, and went back once more to the little three-legged stool by the fire. Then she turned her back on Hester and the young sailor, and went on spreading out her hands to the warmth, as though she could never take the chill off.

"Don't mind her," whispered Hester to her cousin. "She's taking it hard, and I didn't know as it were in her. But presently she'll cry, and that'll bring her round. You tell me what your prospects are, Will. I'm loathe to part with ye, lad, and that's the truth."

"I'll be back by the summer, Hetty. We're going to Africa and back. I'm to be well paid, and it's a good ship to sail in. The cap'n ain't one of your rough and ready, and the rations are fair."

As he spoke he glanced again at Bet, who was leaning her cheek on her hand. Neither he nor Hester could catch any reflection of her face, which was completely hidden.

"We'll talk to her presently," whispered the elder woman. "Now push the table aside, Will, and let's have a sailor-song together, just for good luck."

"No, let's sing 'Barbara Allen,'" said Will. Again he glanced at Bet, and this time he sighed.

The two voices blended well, Will's being of nearly as rare a quality as his cousin's. When they sang, so great was the power of this gift bestowed upon them, they rose several degrees in the scale of refinement and even of education. Their voices lost all trace of dialect, their eyes shone with true feeling. The pathetic old words had never been more fitly rendered.

As the voices rose and swelled, and filled the little room with a perfect melody of sound, Bet ceased to sigh; her hands fell idly into her lap, and her face, which was now turned towards the singers, became filled with a sort of ecstasy. Her parted lips seemed scarcely to breathe, and her eyes reflected the emotions caused by the pathos of the story and the wonderful power of the singers like a mirror.

Will, who was watching her even more intently than Hester, now began to sing only for her. He looked directly at her; and a great many emotions surging in his own soul must have come to her just now, borne on the words of the old ballad -

When he was dead and laid in grave,
Her heart was struck with sorrow.
O mother, mother, make my bed,
For I must die to-morrow.

Farewell, she said, ye virgins all,
And shun the fault I fell in;
Henceforth, take warning by the fall
Of cruel Barbara Allen.

There was almost a note of warning in Will's voice. It died away with a quaver which might have been a reproach.

Bet roused herself with a shivering sigh. "Eh," she said, "she was a cruel one. That was beautiful, Hester. Better than a drink of water when you are thirsty." She raised her hand to wipe away two tears which had rolled down her cheeks.

"It seems to me," she added, "that there is nought in all the world like the music of a grand voice like yours, Hester. It's the only beautiful thing I ha' met - your voice and Will's; they are just grand and summut to be thanked for. Well, I am obliged to you both; but I must say 'goodnight' now, for it is time for me to be going."

"No, no - that you won't, honey," said Hester, bustling forward, and pushing Bet down again on to the three-legged stool. "You're better, and the ice is broke a bit, and you must just set there in that cosy corner and tell me your plans. Oh, you need not mind Will; he'll just smoke his pipe and not listen more than he need to."

"I'll go out if you like," said Will, half rising.

Bet raised her pathetic eyes to his face. "I don't mind you, Will," she said, simply. Her words sent a thrill through the young fellow's heart. He did not know that when she began to speak to Hester she almost forgot his presence.

"Yes, Hester. They ain't much of plans, but such as they be they're made. Mother will be buried come Saturday, and then the boys and me we go away. Father have had fair warning, and he knows me. I'll take the littl'uns and be the best sort of mother I can to them; father shan't have 'em. He kick'd the Cap'n last week - he shan't never do it no more. I promised mother, so there's no argufying on that point - the boys and me we must go."

"But where will you take them, honey? You must find a place where he can't follow you - he's sartin sure to do his best if he thinks you are 'arning money, and I suppose the littl'uns are insured for - same as most of the children around."

"Oh, yes," said Bet, with a short, grim laugh; "he have a price on both their lives - don't let's talk of it. He shan't find 'em - and they shall live, if only to spite him."

"But where will you take 'em, my dear? He's a bad, cruel man, but he is a rare and clever one too, and he will outwit a slip of a lass like you. If he wants the boys he can claim them, I suppose. I'm main sorry for you, Bet; but I don't see how you are to hide them - I really don't."

"I have promised mother," said Bet; "there is no use argufying on that point." Then she added, in a softer

L. T. Meade

voice: "I'm going to the Irish quarter. I know a woman there who'll be a match for father, but I'd best not say her name, for if he comes questioning it is better no one should know. Now, I'll say 'good-night' Hester; thank you for bringing me home. I'm more comforted than I wor."

When Bet rose, Will knocked the ashes out of his pipe. "I'll see you home, Bet," he said; and the two went out together.

When they got out on to the docks, Will said, half slyly, "The night's quite fair; will you come with me, Bet, and I'll show you where the 'Good Queen Anne' is lying at anchor, and all as trim as possible, ready to sail to-morrow night?"

"The 'Good Queen Anne,'" repeated Bet, "that's your ship, ain't it, Will?"

"Why, of course; didn't you hear me tell Hester? I am rare and lucky, I can tell you, to have found a berth in her - good pay and good rations, and a jolly crew, and a fair-spoken captain. It ain't every fellow has the luck to find a berthlike mine. And I'll be back in the summer, Bet. It's a short voyage, and everything just to my mind. You'll wish me luck, won't you, Bet? for the sake of - well, because we used to be playmates a while back, you mind."

"A good while back," repeated Bet. "Oh, yes, I wish you luck, Will. And is that the 'Good Queen Anne?' What is the figure at her bows?"

"A girl," said Will, eagerly, "with her arms over her head and a smile on her lips. Some people say it's a sort of figure of Queen Anne, after whom the ship is named, but I don't take her to be that; and now in the moonlight - you can see her well now, Bet, in the moonlight - with the smile showing upon her lips, she looks like what I take her to be more than ever."

"And what is that, Will?"

"Hope - aye, lass, a right good hope - and luck to Will Scarlett comes in the bonny ship." Bet sighed. Will's blue eyes were looking at her in the moonlight.

"I'll go home now," she said, gently. She sighed again, and half turned away her head from her companion.

"There's a many people have things to be thankful for," she said, presently. "I ain't one of them. I think I'll wish you good-night now, Will. Good-night, and - yes, good luck." She turned away without even offering her hand, plunging suddenly down a narrow court which would lead her out into the front of the town nearest to her home.

Will hesitated for a second; then, the blood surging up into his face, and his heart beating quickly, he ran after her.

"Bet," he cried. "Bet!" He heard her footsteps hurrying faster and faster on ahead of him. Presently, hearing his step, she began to run. He raced after her; he was fleeter than she was, and caught her up by the lamp-post round the corner.

"What did you do that for?" he said to her, almost angrily. "You had no call to give me the slip in that fashion. I hadn't said my say."

"I wanted to get home," said Bet - "the boys will be waiting for their supper, and I have nothing more to talk about."

"But I have," said Will, resolutely - "just a few words, Bet; they won't take long. I made up my mind long ago, only I did not think I'd speak until I had summut to offer. Now I have nought but the name of an honest fellow - only that seems better than nothing at all. Bet, will you wed me if I can manage it afore I sail in the 'Good Queen Anne'?"

Bet looked up with an angry flash in her red-brown eyes.

"Are you mad, Will Scarlet?" she said, "My mother's lying dead, and your ship sails to-morrow night."

"No matter that. If a parson, or the registry office, or any power on God's earth, can make us man and wife to-morrow, Bet why shouldn't we be mated? You have no one in all the world to look after you. There ain't a braver nor a more lone lass in all Liverpool, and I love you with all the strength of my heart. Why shouldn't it be better for me to be your mate than to have no one to take your part, Bet? The voyage will soon be made, and I'll come back with money in my pocket, and while I'm away your father cannot do much agin you if you have wed with me."

All the time Will was talking Bet walked faster and faster. When he had done speaking, however, she had relaxed her steps. They had reached a comparatively deserted place, and, to his surprise and ecstasy, Will felt her lay a timid hand on his arm.

"But I don't love you," she said, sorrowfully.

"You wouldn't want to mate with a girl what didn't love you, Will."

Will caught her hand and held it tightly between both his own.

"There's nought that I mind, except to be a bit of use to you just now, Bet," he said. "You are the lonest lass in this city, and it would be a sight better for you to be wed to me. You ain't afeard, are you? I'll be faithful to you to my dying day, and we have known each other since we were little tots."

"Yes," said Bet, slowly, "and mother liked you, and you can sing fit to wile any lass' heart away; but I don't love you, Will, and I swore long ago that I'd never, never wed."

"You'd never wed?" repeated Will. "There's more lads than me would have a word to say agin that. You ask twenty honest fellows who has the straightest step and bonniest face in the town, and they'd say fast enough it was Bet Granger. You are but joking me when you talk in that fashion, Bet."

"No, Will, it is true. It's a vow I made, and it's my way not to go back of things. When I looked at mother, and see'd the way father treated her, I made up my mind never to wed with none. I'll be no man's mate, and I'll trust myself to none. Good-night, Will, You mean it kindly; and I'd like to ask God, if I was sure that He was there at all, to bless you. Good-night, goodnight."

CHAPTER V.

As Will Scarlett walked home to the small room which he occupied, not very far from his cousin Hester Wright, he was overtaken by a young sailor of about his own age, who linked his arm in his and spoke to him in a half-tipsy, half-jocular voice.

"You was going to give me the slip, Will. And where be you off to at this hour of night?"

"To bed, and to sleep," said Will, shortly. He was in no mood for his companion's idle chatter, and resented the firm grip he had taken of his arm.

"Then it ain't true what I heard," said Isaac Dent. "You're down on your luck, and a bit crusty; and you wouldn't be that ef the news were true."

"What news?" said Will "I'm tired, and that's the truth, Dent. I want to turn in early; for most like I'll be on the briny ocean this time to-morrow."

"Then you are going in the 'Good Queen Anne.' Never knew such a fellow! The best ship in the docks, and you to get a berth in her. I wouldn't be crusty to a less lucky mate if I was in your shoes."

Will sighed. They had come in front of a

brilliantly-lighted public-house, and a flood of gaslight lit up both faces. For a sailor Will was tall, slenderly built, with dark clustering curling hair, and very bright, very honest blue eyes. His companion was short and thick-set - he had a flat head, large ears set rather higher up, and small cunning eyes. He was not pleasant-looking, and Will, although one of the most unsuspicious of mortals, regarded him with small favor.

"Come in, and have a parting drink for good luck," said Dent, pointing to the gaily-lit public house.

Will shook his hand from his arm.

"You know my mind on that point," he said. "We took a voyage together, so we needn't talk it all out now. Good-night, Dent, I'm off to bed."

But Dent had no idea of letting Will off so easy.

"Look here," he said - "what shall I pay you for that berth of your'n? It ain't nothing to the cap'n who sails with him, and I wants to get away. What will you take?"

Will felt his face flushing; then he laughed indignantly.

"What folly you talk, Dent. Even suppose I were willing, you haven't sixpence - you know you haven't."

"May I go home with you?" said Dent, "and I'll show you what I have. I'm in real earnest - I want to get away, and I can pay for it. The 'Good Queen Anne' is quite to my mind - time for sailing, length of voyage - all just what I wants. I'll give you ten pound if you'll drop that berth of yours in my favor. There - I can't speak fairer than that."

All the time Dent was speaking Will had walked on stoically. There was not the faintest appearance of wavering about him; but Dent, who was a shrewd observer of character, and knew this particular young sailor well, guessed that Will's teeth were set hard, and that there was a struggle going on in his breast.

"May I come home with you, mate," he said, "just for a bit, to talk the matter over quiet like? I ha' got ten pound - no matter how and no matter where - and it's yours just to let me go to sea this week instead of next. A handy, neat-looking sailor like you, Will, need never be long out of a berth, and it's vital for me to get away just now. Ten pound, just to oblige a mate! You won't get such an offer again in a hurry, Scarlett."

"Stop!" said Will, suddenly. "What child is that? I'll be back with you in a minute if you'll wait by the corner, Dent, but I must follow up that littl'un - he have no call to be out at this hour."

Will made a step or two forward, and found himself in the midst of a small crowd who were admiring the antics of a very small and grotesque performer. A little boy with reddish hair and blackened face was turning somersaults with wonderful rapidity in the centre of the pathway. Another boy, cap in hand, stood by his side. The boy who performed and the boy who begged both looked audacious and disreputable; but, owing to their tiny statures, and the cadaverous whiteness of their faces, there was something pathetic in the spectacle. The boy who stood with his cap waiting for stray half-pence or pence to be dropped into it, had large blue eyes, which were turned with marvelous rapidity, first in the direction of one spectator, then in that of another. He could pick out the people who were hopeful, and whose purse-strings were likely to be loosened, with the swiftest of glances; and his little cap received many doles, considering the nature of the crowd who looked on.

Dent, who had come up to Will, tossed the boy a half-penny, and then began to laugh heartily, at the rapid contortions of the little acrobat.

"Stop that!" said Will, angrily.

He stepped into the middle of the crowd, and caught the revolving boy suddenly by his shoulder.

"You have no call to be out at this hour, Nat - nor you neither, Thady. What will your sister say when she finds you not in? Bad boys - run home this minute. This ain't what your mother would have liked; and you know it."

The boy called Thady, otherwise the captain, raised his blue eyes, now swimming in tears, to Will's face.

"We was that 'nngry," he said. "And Bet were out. Yer's a lot of coppers; we'll do now. Come along home, Gen'ral."

The two scampered away, flying with their bare feet along the slippery streets, and in a moment were out of sight.

Dent stared hard at Will, whose face showed some agitation.

"So those are the two little Granger lads," he said. "Well, I tell you what-their sister's far and away the handsomest girl in Liverpool."

"She's well enough," said Will, shortly. "The boys had no call to be out so late - and to-night of all nights. Their mother is lying dead, and Bet's in trouble. Good-night, Dent. I ha' made up my mind to sail in the `Good Queen Anne.' I won't trouble you to come home with me, although I'm obleeged for your offer."

The light was falling on Will's face. Dent looked up at him sharply.

"So Bet Granger's mother is dead," he said. "Well, she's a handsome lass. I mean to marry her, if I can, arter next voyage."

"Ef you can," said Will.

Dent noticed his violent stand, and then the quick restraint he put upon himself.

"Yes," repeated Dent. "And her father's willing, for I spoke to him. I'll marry her arter this voyage, or maybe I'll marry her afore, ef you don't let me buy your berth from you, Will. Come, shall I go home with you? Any one with half an eye can see that you have no mind for the ocean wave just at present. Let's come in, Scarlett - we're close to your lodgings now - and finger the bit of gold I ha' by me as comfortable as we please."

"You worry a fellow almost to death," said Will; but he made no further objection, and the two went up to Will's tiny bedroom at the top of a tall house.

They were closted together for about an hour. At the end of that time Dent came downstairs whistling triumphantly, but with a very ugly look about his face. He had bought a berth on board the "Good Queen Anne" for two crisp Bank of Englandfive-pound notes, but the loss of the money seemed to cause him more relief than otherwise.

"And don't you think, Scarlett, that you'll get the girl either," he said to himself, "for I mean to have her for myself. And if this little trick hasn't checkmated you, my fine lad, I'll find summut else to spoil your bit of a game."

Upstairs Will was fingering the paper money, with a queer dazed expression on his face.

What had he done? Given up his berth on the bonny ship, and his chance of a voyage after his own heart - given it up, too, for Isaac Dent, a fellow whom he was quite sure was more or less a bit of a scoundrel. Will was honest, unsuspicious, and guileless; but even he could not quite think the best of a man with Dent's physiognomy.

"And I care nought at all for the money," he said to himself. "Only maybe it 'ud come in handy, if she wor to wed me 'twixt this week and next. *He* shan't have her with his ugly face. But she wouldn't look at him. She said to-night that it worn't for her ever to wed, but maybe as I can bring her round. I'll find another berth next week, and I'll speak to Hester to-morrow, and a deal can be done in a week. She said she didn't love me, but - who knows? Bet's a wild one, and a desperate earnest one. Ef she could bring herself to say just once, 'I love you, Will.' it 'ud be as good from her as if she said it every day. It's once and always with Bet. Well, I shouldn't ha' stayed now ef Dent hadn't let out that he meant to make up to her. Dent shan't cross her path if I can help it. She's the bravest lass in Liverpool, and the handsomest to look at; and I'll have her, if fortune will favor me, and the good God above help me. 'I don't love you, Will,' she said; but for that matter, Barbara Allen said much the same, and yet she died for love arter all. When I think of that, and remember how Bet's eyes lit up, and how pitiful she looked, when I sang of Barbara Allen, I ain't sorry as Dent has got my berth. A week off the ocean wave ain't too much to give up for the sake of Bet Granger."

CHAPTER VI.

Hester Wright was a popular, but by no means, in the usual acceptance of the word, a specially good woman. She was the reverse of strait-laced; her morals were nothing in particular, and her ideas on all subjects, whether on righteousness or wickedness, the broadest of the broad. She went neither to church nor chapel on Sundays - she professed no religion, although when pressed on the point she would not admit that it worn't there. "May be it wor," she would say, only she had no time for it just now. She did not blame people for going to the public-house, although she never went herself, simply because that special place did not suit her special temperament; but she was extremely fond of spending her evenings at the penny theatres, or other cheap and decidedly low places of entertainment. There she would enjoy herself, looking on with eager interest at the coarse and gaudy representations of so-called "life." She would never laugh loudly, however, or applaud noisily, although she encouraged and smiled at those who did. She was very poor, but she was always neat in her person; and the expression in her big black eyes gave her a look a little above her station, so that, although she was not handsome, those who saw her once often turned to glance at her again. Wherever she went, in whatever company she found herself, she was invariably good-natured. Indeed, although she was not in the least aware of the fact, she

L. T. Meade

was a most unselfish person. If a tired-out and hard-worked mother was seen pushing her way to the front at Hester's favorite theatre, The Cleopatra, Hester invariably resigned her own seat in her favor, and took the baby and amused it while the mother looked on and laughed. For girls and boys, particularly girls and boys who were sweethearting, she had a strong sympathy, getting them together in a very quiet and unobtrusive manner, and taking the keenest pleasure in promoting their happiness. She was extremely popular with the Liverpool girls, and this popularity was the great delight of her life. The girl who would not go near the parson or the Sunday-school teacher, or the Sister of Mercy, would pour out her woes or her joys into Hester's sympathetic ears - would receive the advice Hester gave, eagerly, and as a rule, if it were palatable or not, act upon it. No handsome young girl had the least cause to be jealous of Hester; for although she was still comparatively young, and had a power of attraction accorded to few women, it was well known in Hester's very wide circle of indiscriminate acquaintances that she had long ago vowed a vow, far more solemn than Bet's in her ignorance, to take to herself no mate, and to share her life with no one. Hester's mate that shou'd have been had gone away far over the ocean and never come back again. He had been drowned at sea; and although she made no fuss and paraded her sorrow before no one, yet other men saw it would be useless to think of her as a wife. She was not aparticularly industrious woman, and was perfectly indifferent to the comforts of life. She kept her room clean and neat, because, notwithstanding the queer medley which her character presented, she had certain refinements about her, cropping up in all sorts of queer directions - one of them lay in her great regard for personal neatness, the other in her wonderful gift of song. Hester could laugh at a coarse joke, but it was quite impossible for her to lend her voice to singing a coarse song. She liked old ballads best, and her choice of music was quite wonderful for a person of her education. If she had a strong love or passion it was for popularity. She liked to see the young lads or lasses crowding around her, begging for a song, or asking her for advice or help of any kind. She was a good worker, and got plenty to do from one of the beet boys' outfitting shops in Castle Street; but she was always extremely poor, and often knew what it was to be hungry, for she gave her money away quite as fast as she earned it. Her beautiful voice, although only used for the benefit of the lowest of the people, had brought to her more than one offer of lucrative employment from the managers of music-halls and cheap theatres. But Hester would have nothing to say to such proposals.

"I ain't keen about money," she would answer, "and I won't sell my voice. Somehow, it would take the joy out of it."

On the night after Hester had taken Bet home, she found herself in the entrance of The Cleopatra Theatre, about seven o'clock. A new piece was to be put on the stage that night, and the entrance to the small pit was already crowded with rough men and frowsy, untidy, disreputable girls. They all nodded to Hester, and seemed pleased to see her, and one or two made way to get her to the front.

"My Jack is coming presently, Hetty," whispered a girl of the name of Susan Jakes. "Set near me, like a dear, so as to keep a seat for him when he looks in."

Hester often performed this kind office, slipping quietly into the background afterwards, without permitting any word of thanks. Susan Jakes was a pale-faced girl, with light flaxen hair and pale blue eyes; she was rather pretty and very neglected-looking. When she saw "my Jack" her somewhat hard little face assumed a womanly and beautiful expression. Hester took her hand and gave it a squeeze.

"We'll keep side by side until Jack Masters comes," she whispered.

The girl and Hester, by reason of Hester's great popularity, got into quite a foremost position in the pit. Jack Masters arrived about half-an-hour afterwards, and just before the curtain was raised. He scarcely thanked Hetty - it was the usual thing for her to keep seats for the girl's sweethearts. She moved aside into quite the back of the crowded pit, and stood leaning against the wall. A dreadfully tired-looking woman touched her arm.

"I've got out, Hetty Wright - he's at the public, and I'm here. Ain't it fine?"

"What have you done with the children?" asked Hester. "Yes, I'm glad you're in for a bit of pleasure, Mrs. Jones."

"See," said Mrs. Jones, pushing aside her shawl with a triumphant smile, "you overlooked her, the crowd's so great, but little Sarah's here. I put the others to bed, and neighbor Bryce will feed Tommy if he cries; but I brought little Sal along o' me. My! ain't she peart with delight? We're both that starved to see a bit of real gentry life, and to hear a good song or two."

Sal was a very minute maiden of eight years of age. Her whole small face was radiant with anticipation, but she could see nothing over the heads of the crowd. Instantly Hester lifted her into her arms.

"Lean on me, Sal," she said, "and look your fill. See, the curtain is up, and the play is going to begin."

It was a new piece and alas! only half prepared. A wretched performance it would have been at its best, badly put on, badly acted - coarse, common, the reverse of all that was lifelike; but, nevertheless, these eager, hungry, expectant people would have been abundantly content with the most extravagant representations if they had only been carried on with the smallest show of life or spirit. The actors, however, who none of them knew their parts, struggled on miserably for a scene or two, and then broke down utterly. It does not cost much to go to a penny theatre, but the people who frequent such places are, of all those in the world, the most anxious to get their money's worth. There was instantly an uproar and a clamor, and the house resounded with hisses, which but for a small incident would quickly have broken into yells.

The incident was this: Just when the piece was wavering to its miserable and final crash, Hester felt some hot, soft tears dripping on her face.

"I don't like it," said little Sal, "And they don't sing. I'm hungry to hear 'em sing - I'm hungry to hear 'em sing just one song."

"Yes, it's a biting disappointment," whispered the mother. "Sal ha' been telling of nothing else all day.

She'd give all the world to hear jest a song, and it seems to me as they can't do nothing - not even speak."

Just then the crash came. The curtain was lowered, and the manager, purple in the face, came hastily and eagerly to the front. Little Sal put her head down on Hester's neck and wept bitterly, and then began the hisses and the cries of "Shame!"

"Never mind, Sal - I'll sing to you," whispered Hester. Quick as thought her resolve was taken. She was not the least self-conscious, but she was full of pity for the people. If every child in the room - and there were several - wanted a song as badly as Sal did, she could satisfy the small disappointed hearts.

She pushed her way through the crowd, saying to each who tried to hinder her -

"Let me pass, I'll sing to you; you know I can sing."

Her words were caught up, and cheers for Hester Wright ran through the house from her friends - and most there knew her, and were her friends - long before she reached the wings, and joined the astonished manager, who stood wavering, and in a considerable state of terror, on his deserted stage.

"I'll sing," said Hester, speaking to him eagerly and quickly. "The children are bitterly disappointed, and a song or two will quiet the whole house. Let me; I know how."

The manager was a stranger in the town, and had no acquaintance with the dark-eyed, intense woman who addressed him. The crowd, however, cheered and vociferated. Their ill-humor was changed into the most hearty approval.

"Just like Hetty, bless her," whispered Susan Jakes to her sweetheart. "Just like Hetty," resounded all over the small house. Be the woman mad or not, the manager saw she was popular, and his brow cleared.

"Yes, sing - sing anything," he responded, in a voice of intense relief. "I'll pay you anything in reason - only sing, and keep them quiet. This is an awful minute for me."

"I'll sing for the children, and not for money," said Hester, flashing an angry glance at him; and then her magnificent voice arose, and filled the house.

For some reason, the ballad which she and her cousin had sung together for Bet the night before was still ringing in her head. It rose easily to her lips, and she sang it first, giving point and meaning to the words in a way which took the manager by storm. What would he not give to secure such a treasure as Hester Wright for his house? "Home, sweet Home," came next; and then why she could not tell, perhaps because of a pain which was tugging at her heart, perhaps because of the weary look on some of the faces, and because a whole tide of memories was thronging before her, she chose "The Land o' the Leal." Such words, such melody, had never been heard before in that penny theatre. The women looked wistful, and many of them wept. Hester seemed to sing straight into their very hearts. The men shuffled uneasily, and one or two of them wiped their rough hands across their eyes.

"And oh, we'll all meet

L. T. Meade

In the Land o' the Leal."

sang Hester, and then her voice died away, and she turned and whispered something to the manager and hastily disappeared.

The men and women went home quietly; tender and long-forgotten feelings had been briefly aroused, and very few who had visited The Cleopatra went near the public-house that night.

"Them was blessed words," whispered little Sal's mother, "and she's a blessed gel. Talk of saints, I call Hester Wright one, though she never preached no sarmon. The 'Land o' the Leal' - why, it's there as our Johnny's gone. Bless her heart! The world ain't quite without comfort, when one thinks of bits of words like them."

CHAPTER VII.

Hester was excited and overwrought; she could not meet any of the crowd, and took refuge in one of the deserted wings, until, as she hoped, every one had dispersed. As she was quietly leaving the wings she was met, much to her annoyance, by the manager. He was a coarse, florid-faced person, but he took off his hat to Hester, as if she had been the finest lady in the land.

"I thank you most heartily," he said. "You have saved me - you have saved the house. Now, what shall I give you? A pound, two pounds? I'll give them to you - yes, gladly; and I'll engage that you come here every night at a fair salary. What's your address, my good girl, and what's your name? You've got a voice to be proud of, and that I will say."

"I told you I would not sing for money," said Hester, angrily. "Good-night, sir. I'm glad I gave the children and the women a bit of pleasure, but my voice ain't to be bought for no money. You ain't the first as has wanted it, but it ain't for you. Good-night, sir. I'm sorry as you think so little of the people what come here. They have hard lives, and they want their bit of pleasure, and you shouldn't take their money, what ain't easy to get, ef you have nothing to show them for it. I sang for the people to-night, not for you. My voice

L. T. Meade

and me, we belong to the poor folk of Liverpool. Good-night, sir-you have nought to thank me for."

She rushed out of the open door, not heeding the manager's outstretched hand, nor the raised tones with which he sought still to detain her. It was late now, nearly eleven o'clock, and the public-houses would be closed in about a quarter of an hour. A miserable old dame stood shivering by one, and looking wistfully into the warm and brilliantly lighted place. She turned her wan and wretched face round when she heard Hester approaching.

"Good-night, Hetty Wright, and may the Virgin bless you!" she called out.

"Good-night, Mrs. Flannigan - why, how white and starved you look! Here's twopence; go in and get a drop of gin."

Hester dropped the coins into the old dame's hand, and hurried quickly through the damp streets.

The wretched woman gazed at them in a kind of petrifaction. Twopence from a girl as poor as herself, and she was to buy gin with the money? Gin! Never before had she been told to go and buy gin. Why, the missionaries, and all the good folks round, said it was the curse of the land. And so it was: had it not brought her to what she was? Had it not sent her only son to an untimely grave? Oh, yes - none knew better than mother Flannigan what gin meant - what cursing and what tears, and what misery it had caused; and yet the girl with the white face and the great dark earnest wistful eyes had given her twopence to buy it, and told her to get warm and comforted. Oh, yes, gin was bad, but it was very comforting; she would have her two-pennyworth, and she would go home, and forget her hunger, and sleep comfortably all night. It was really good of that decent, pale-faced girl to give her two-pence to spend in gin. She knew her: she was the girl with the voice, the girl about whom some of the neighbors, even in the Irish quarter, raved.

With the memory of Hester's face firmly fixed on her dazed old brain, Mother Flannigan entered the public-house. Then a queer thing happened. By the side of Hester's pure, highly-wrought face arose the picture of another - of a very suffering, thirsty little grandchild, who lay waiting for her on a bed of straw at home. Instantly the desire for gin departed - the old woman purchased instead two-pennyworth of very blue and watery milk, and hurried away to give her grandson a drink.

When Hester reached her lodgings the overwrought mood was still upon her. She lit her fire, however, and put the kettle on to boil. Then, throwing aside her hat and thin black cashmere shawl, she sat down beside her little deal table, placed her elbows on it, and stared hard before her. Just at that moment she was suffering acutely - a tumult of mingled feelings possessed her; she was unsatisfied, and longing for she knew not what. A weaker woman in such a mood would have relieved her overcharged brain with a flood of tears. Instead of crying, Hester sang. For a woman with no religion, and no belief in religion, the queerest words arose to her lips. She had sometimes listened outside the churches to the swelling organs and the music of the choirs; once, when an anthem was being very exquisitely rendered, she had stolen fascinated inside the church porch. Now the words of this anthem came to her lips, and floated on her splendid voice through the dreary little attic room:

"Oh, rest in the Lord; wait patiently for him - patiently for him; and he will give thee thy heart's - thy heart's desire."

There came a knock at the door, and Hester sprang to her feet.

"Come in," she said. And Will Scarlet stepped into the room.

"Why, Hetty, how lovely you are making the night with that voice of yourn. I didn't rightly catch the words nor the air - what were they?"

"Oh, words I picked up, Will. It's a way of mine never to lose either words or air that take my fancy. But what are you doing in my room, Will Scarlet? I thought you'd be miles away on the waves, in the 'Good Queen Anne,' by now."

"And I wish I were, Hetty. But I've a bit of a yarn to spin on that head. May I sit by your fire for a bit and say my say?"

"To be sure, Will. And you shall have a cup of tea with me, I'm just making a brew. I expect I were a bit lonely at the thought of your being so far away, cousin; and I'll say frankly I'm real glad to have you sitting again by my fireside."

Will smiled. His likeness to Hetty was very marked at this moment, more particularly so as on his usually careless and almost boyish face there sat an unusual cloud of perplexity and trouble.

"The fact is, Het-I may as well have it all out at once-
I'm in a bit of a taking. I had a talk with Bet Granger
last night, and I offered to wed her. I didn't see how
she could do better than to give herself to me. I has set
my heart on her for years, and I thought it would be a
kind of a help to her ef she had my name to hold on by,
even if I were away at sea. And so I thought we might
be wed as soon as ever a parson could tie us up. I
hadn't much to offer her, but I were real in earnest, and
she could see it."

"Yes, Will; and what did she say?"

Hester had dropped on one knee, and was gazing
intently into her cousin's face.

"Oh, she flouted me, Hetty - said she had vowed to
wed no one, and all that sort of thing. Poor Bet - she
have sperrit of her own, and life have never gone easy
with her. She seemed to think she was sorry for me.
She makes out that she's all as hard as brass, but she
ain't really."

"No, she ain't really," repeated Hester. "It's all a kind
of cloak. I ha' used it myself, but Bet overdoes it. Ef
ever there's a girl with a great warm heart it's Bet
Granger."

Will's eyes were shining at the words of praise.

"God bless you, Hetty!" he said.

Hester looked at him anxiously.

"Poor lad! And she wouldn't have nought to do with you? I'm sorry for you, Will, but Bet ain't the girl not to know her own mind. Ef she refused you, lad, why didn't you join the crew of the 'Good Queen Anne'? It ain't best for a lad like you to be loafing about Liverpool. I'm main sorry you ha' lost your berth in the good ship, Will."

"You must hear me out, Hester. I haven't half told my yarn."

Then Will related what befell him the night before-how Dent walked home with him, and begged to buy his place in the ship; how Will was firm in his refusal until Dent declared his intention of going in for Bet, and making her his wife at any cost.

"He shan't have her," said Will, clenching his fist. "A fellow like Dent!-why, he's a real bad 'un, Hester. Why, he swears dreadful, and he drinks deep, and he's cruel. Ef you had seen how he treated the cabin boy when we was mates together in the `Betsy Prig' you wouldn't like the feel of knowing that a girl what you loved more than all the world should even set eyes on him. Why, he's a worse man than Bet's father, and that's saying enough."

"Yes, it's saying enough," said Hester. "And so you sold your berth to Isaac?"

"Yes-I wanted to get rid of him, and I can soon find another. Liverpool's a bit a fresher place to-night because he's not in it."

"And what did he give you, Will?"

"Ten pounds, in Bank of England notes. I have them in my pocket. Shall I show them to you, Hester?"

"No, no; only keep them close. Don't talk of them, and don't change them until you can't help yourself. This is a bad part of town for a lad to have a bit of money in. You keep your lips sealed about it, Will - that is, if you want to keep the money."

"Never fear," said Will. "I think I have sold my berth for mighty little."

Hester rose from her place by the fire. She began to pour the boiling water into her little cracked teapot, and now she placed it on the hob to draw.

"What floors me, Will, is this," she said, - "how did a fellow like Dent come by so much money? Ef there is a ne'er-do-well it's Dent; and I want to know how he come by a lot of money like that."

"I can't tell you," replied Will. "I suppose he was well paid after his last voyage. He's a prime seaman, whatever else he ain't. He'd a bit of gold or two in his pocket, and some silver besides the notes - yes, now I come to think of it, he was remarkably flush of coin for a chap like him."

"Well, you hold by the notes, Will, and don't change them afore you need. I suppose you'll be looking out for another berth now you have lost that in the 'Good Queen Anne'?"

"All in good time, Hester. I mean to wed Bet Granger first,"

"But you can't, Will, if the girl has no mind to have you."

"I mean to wed her," replied Will, in a dogged, resolute sort of voice. "Ef she has a heart - and I know she has a heart - she shall give it to me; and she shall love me, yes, as well - as well as I love her. Why, Hetty, that fellow Dent said that her father was on his side, and would help him to get Bet. Do you think arter that I'd leave Liverpool before I made her my lawful wife?"

CHAPTER VIII.

In due course Mrs. Granger received a decent burial. There was money enough for this purpose in the burial club to which Granger subscribed; and Bet, rather to her surprise, saw that her father did not object to doing the thing respectably for his dead wife. She and the little boys and Granger himself, who was quite sober and looked remarkably sulky, attended the funeral. The short service was quickly over, and the queer-looking band of mourners turned away. As they were leaving the cemetery, a thick-set and ungainly man, with eyes closely set in his head, and a hat slouched over his forehead, came up and spoke to Granger.

"All right, Dent," said Granger.

Then he turned to his daughter.

"You know Isaac Dent, don't you, Bet? You might ha' the manners to give him a civil word."

Bet's eyes were red and swollen, for she had been crying bitterly.

"Oh, yes, I know you, Isaac Dent," she said; "but I ain't in no mood to talk now. Good-bye, father."

"I'll be home presently," called out Granger. "Have a

L. T. Meade

bit of dinner ready for Dent and me-we'll be looking in presently;" and Bet, taking a small brother by each hand, walked away at a good pace.

She had not replied to her father, and there was a very dogged, determined look on her handsome face. The two small boys chattered to one another, looked proudly down at their boots, which had been bought new for the occasion, and often glanced at Bet. She did not pay the slightest heed to their shrill childish chatter. Presently she hailed a passing tramcar, and delighted her little brothers by taking them for a ride outside. The three got down at the nearest point to Sparrow Street, which was the name of Bet's old address. They reached the house and went upstairs. The one room where they had all lived for the last couple of years looked deserted, ugly, desolate. The bed on which the dead woman had lain was empty, the fire was out in the grate, and the broken cups and saucers, out of which the little party had breakfasted before they started for the funeral, stood unwashed on the deal table.

"Now, boys," said Bet, the minute she had got the two little fellows into the room, "you ha' got to obey me. I'm your mother in future. Do you mind?"

She had seated herself on a low chair, and drew her little brothers in front of her. They looked at her with their impudent and bright eyes.

"The Cap'n says," began Nat, glancing in his eager, quick, bird-like way at his brother - "the Cap'n says -"

But Bet put her hand across the eager little mouth.

"Never mind what Thady says now, Nat; we'll have plenty of time to go into that by-and-bye. Now we have a deal to do, and very little time to do it in. But first you two boys ha' got to give me a promise."

"Promises is like pie-crusts," said the Cap'n, drawing himself up to his full tiny height, "I don't mind, nor do the Gen'ral there. Promises is made to be broke."

Bet shook the little speaker impatiently.

"Look here, boys, there's no one loves you two, but me; and I do - yes, I do - with all my heart. There, boys, don't strangle me," for they both fell upon her, covering her face and neck and lips with childish, most affectionate kisses.

"Hurrah for Bet! There, Bet - we'll make no pie-crust promises to you. We'll promise, and we'll keep our words. We'd die afore we broke 'em!" concluded the Cap'n, stamping his small newly-shod foot with great effect on the floor.

"There's no one loves you but me," continued Bet. "Mother did, but she's with God - that is ef - ef - oh, yes, mother's with God. He's keeping her comfortable now, and she have forgot us all. Mother's no good from this out; and father - you know what father is, boys. Look me in the face - you know what father is."

It took a great deal to quench the spirit of the audacious Granger twins, but they looked subdued now. Their thin little faces grew a shade whiter. The two pairs of eyes gave a rapid glance towards the door, and the little figures pressed closer to Bet as if for protection.

"You know, and so do I," she continued, putting her strong arm round them with a most protecting gesture; "and so - and so - boys, I'm going to take you away from father. And the only thing you ha' got to obey me in is when I say 'hide!' you are to hide; and when I ha' to lock you up, as I may have to do now and then, you won't play no larks on me, nor try to get away."

"No - no!" they both vociferated eagerly. "We promise, we promise true. Hurrah for Bet - the best gel in Liverpool!"

"That'll do; now let's pack. We must be out of this room in ten minutes."

The three flew about, Bet putting her own small possessions and the boys' scanty wardrobe into an old shawl of her mother's. It took far less than ten minutes to make a bundle of the poor possessions. At the last moment Bet went over to the bed, laid her head face downwards on her mother's pillow, and reverently kissed the place where the dead cold head had rested.

"That's a seal to my promise," she whispered; and then, slinging the bundle across her shoulder, she again took the boys' hands and went downstairs.

At the entrance to the house she met her landlord, a man of the name of Bounce.

"Ah, my dear, and where are you off to?" he said, in his most facetious voice.

"I am going away, Mr. Bounce," replied Bet, gravely; "you can tell my father - he'll be in presently - as I ain't a-coming back. Neither me nor the boys is a-coming back. Good-bye."

She did not wait for the landlord's surprised answer, but his rude laugh floated after her down the street.

There are slums and slums in Liverpool, as elsewhere, and Sparrow street, which Bet had left, seemed by contrast to Paradise Row, which she presently entered, a thoroughly respectable, indeed genteel, place of residence. Paradise Row was not very far from the river. It was entered by a court, court of not more than twenty feet square. Under one of the houses there was an archway, and it was only through this archway that any one could approach Paradise Row, This charming and most suitably-named place of residence consisted of twenty houses at one side of the street and twenty at the other. The houses were high, and the street between was not more than ten feet across. There were no pathways, and no apparent drains of any sort. The houses got closer together as they approached the sky, so that it would not be impossible for an agile person in case of pursuit to throw a board across from his window to the one opposite, and so effect an escape. There were not a great many panes of glass in the windows - rags and pieces of board taking the place of this precious commodity. It was an evil-looking-place, and the two little boys, accustomed as they were to a very rough life, looked at Bet in some surprise as she led them there.

"This is a rum go," whispered the general under his breath; but the little blue-eyed captain was silent, drawing himself up very erect, and trying to imitate his sister's stately carriage.

Presently Bet paused at a door, and went in.

L. T. Meade

"Is Mother Bunch in her room?" she asked a red-haired unkempt-looking boy, who, with a short pipe in his mouth, was leaning against the doorway. He did not trouble himself to remove the pipe, but pointed in the direction of a certain door. Bet went forward, and opened it without knocking. A very stout woman of between fifty and sixty was standing before a wash-tub. Her arms were bare to the elbows, and covered with suds. Her blue winsey petticoat was tucked up above her ankles; her large feet were destitute of shoes and stockings. She had a broad face, a snub nose, and two twinkling good-humored eyes. Notwithstanding her dirt-and she was very dirty-the first glance into her face gave one a certain feeling of comfort and confidence. This was curious; for Mother Bunch had the loudest tongue and the most stalwart arm in Paradise Row; she was, in short, the terror of the place and the adjacent neighborhood. Bet, however, approached her without a particle of fear; she knew that Mother Bunch was a good friend as well as a good foe.

"I ha' come," she said, going straight up to her. "And here are the boys. This one is Cap'n, and this one is Gen'ral. They're rare 'uns for fighting, poor lads; and they ain't cowards. Have you got the room for us, Mother Bunch?"

"To be sure, honey," replied Mother Bunch, wiping her arms, and smiling broadly at Bet. "And indeed, and indeed, it's the truth I'm telling you, love, when I say that not a purtier or nicer little room could be found in the whole of the Row. You come along o' me, me dears-oh, and it's chape as dirt you're getting it, love!"

The burly Irishwoman panted and rolled her-self upstairs. Bet came next, carrying her bundle, and the boys followed in the rear. The stairs were slippery, and dark, and broken - full of dangers and pitfalls to all but the most wary.

"Jump across here, love," said Mother Bunch; "there's a hole two feet wide just by this corner, and you'd drop into the cellar ef you worn't careful. Oh, glory! but my breath's nearly gone - I'm bate entirely. I'm letting you the room chape as dirt, Bet Granger, 'cos I've took a fancy to you, honey; and that's as true as my name is Molly O'Flaherty. 'Tis the Irish you have about you here, love - 'tis them as is thrue to the backbone as is your neighbors, dear. Fight for you! honey, - oh, yes, we'll fight. Them boys, why they're Mother Bunch's boys now. There, honey, there's your room, and as purty an attic as heart could wish. A shilling a week! Why, it's chaper than dirt! Now then, I must go back to hang up my bits of duds. There's the kay of the room, love, and Molly O'Flaherty's blessings on all three of yez."

Mother Bunch turned, and thumped and bumped herself downstairs; and Bet, her eyes bright, and a spot of intense color on each of her cheeks, turned round to the boys.

"Look here," she said excitedly - "we're as safe here as if we was in London. Do you think father will come to Paradise Row? and do you think he'll face Mother Bunch? Yes, laddies, the room is small and close, and horrid and dirty; and I *hate* it, but I won't give way, and I won't cry. I've got soap in this bundle, and washing soda, and an old brush, and we'll clean it up - you two and me - and make it fit for mother's boys to live in."

L. T. Meade

The little fellows, who were really frightened, cheered up at these words. The dreadful attic, with its slanting roof and its tiny skylight window, was illuminated by brave, handsome Bet's presence, and by the comforting knowledge that the wretched man who called himself their father could give them no blows nor kicks here. A miserable neighbor in an opposite attic presently heard the three laughing as they worked.

CHAPTER IX.

Soap-and-Water can effect wonders, and by the evening Bet's attic looked like another place. She and the boys had worked with hearty good-will; three pairs of vigorous young arms had removed cobwebs, and scattered dirt, and let in a little fresh air. After all, there were worse rooms in this house than the upstairs unused attic, and the air which blew right down from the sky when Bet opened the tiny window was pure and sweet. The energetic girl had saved all her nightly earnings since her mother's death, and now she had three or four shillings in her pocket. Accompanied by the twins, who looked at her with adoring eyes, she went out presently, and purchased coals and food; and the three that evening, after the fire was lit and the kettle boiled, felt quite sociable and almost festive. Bet's heart was lighter than it had been since her mother's death; she did not despair of doing well for her brothers, and of bringing them up in such a way, and with such a due regard for religion, that by-and-bye they should meet their mother in the land where she now dwelt.

"Ef she's there - ef there is a future, she must have Nat and Thady with her," concluded Bet, as she watched the two small lads polishing off a hearty meal of bread and tea. "That's my part - to train 'em so as they'll choose religion and go to mother by-and-bye."

L. T. Meade

When the meal was over she called the boys to her. "Kneel down now, both of you, and say your prayers," she said. "Say 'Our Father 'chart heaven' and 'Matthew, Mark, Luke, John.'"

"Mother didn't teach us 'Matthew, Mark, Luke and John,'" said the captain.

"Well, love, say what she did teach; and be quick, for I must go out to buy and sell my papers."

The captain and the general knelt down obediently, closed their eyes, folded their hands, and went through the Lord's Prayer in high sing-song chanting voices. Then the general was silent - he opened his eyes and looked impatiently at his brother.

"That's all," he said.

"No, it ain't all," repeated Thady, "I'm a-try-ing to thing - don't keep nudging me, Nat -

'In the kingdom of Thy Grace
Grant a little child a place.'

That's it, yes, that's it - and Nat, shut your eyes and say what I'm saying - ' God bless Bet for ever and ever. Amen.'"

Nat joined in this last clause with hearty goodwill, and Bet felt a queer sensation coming into her throat. She kissed the little boys, locked the door upon them, and went out.

There were no girls in Paradise Row exactly like Bet. In the first place she was clean; in the next, she carried herself like a princess. She was so well made, and her head so beautifully set upon her shoulders, that it was impossible for her to be awkward. Her uncovered head with its wealth of hair shone with a kind of radiance when she passed under any lamp-post. Her lips were finely set, and she glanced scornfully and with a sort of touch-me-not air at any man or woman who happened to look at her with admiration. Her own defiant young steps and her own proud disdainful face were her best protection. Even in this rough Irish quarter no one molested her with an uncivil word. She felt quite hopeful to-night - the little boys' love and confidence cheered her. Thady's short prayer had touched the really great and deep heart which slumbered in her breast.

"I'd die for 'em, poor little chaps," she murmured; and she clenched her hand at the thought of any evil touching them. "Why, it's well I have 'em; there's no one else as cares for Bet Granger."

But then she thought of Will, and as she did so her heart quickened its steady, even pulse. Will wasn't the sort of lad that a girl could say "No" to without a sensation of pain. Bet thought of him as bonny. "He's good - yes, he's good," she murmured, and then she remembered the song of Barbara Allen, and she found herself humming the words which Will had sung in his strong, brave voice -

"When he was dead and laid in grave.
Her heart was broke with sorrow."

"Folly!" said Bet, breaking off abruptly. "It ain't for me to think of no man; and I'm not Barbara Allen, and Will will get another girl to be a good mate for him some day. Poor Will - he's a bonny lad, all the same."

Bet had now reached the place where she purchased her papers. She made her usual careful selection - so many of the *Star*, so many of the *Evening Echo*, so many of the *Herald*. With them tucked under her arm, she soon reached her own special beat, and standing under the lamp-light, with her goods temptingly displayed, had even more than her usual luck. A dark-eyed, bold-looking girl presently came up and spoke to her.

"You seem to be doing a thriving business, Bet," she said, with a laugh.

"Same as usual" answered Bet. "This is about the best beat in Liverpool, and the gentlemen know me. I always give them their papers clean."

Just then a customer came up who wanted an *Evening Echo*. The Echo was a halfpenny paper. He gave Bet a penny, who returned him a halfpenny change. When this customer had departed the black-eyed girl burst into a fit of laughter.

"Well, you *are* a flat, Bet Granger," she said - "the greenest of the green. What can a gent like that want with a ha'penny? When I sells evening papers - and I've made a good thing of them round Lime Street - I never has no change; that's my way."

"Is it?" said Bet. "Well honesty's my way. I've nearly sold my papers now, Louisa, so I'll say 'good-night.'"

"Do tell me what you made first. I ha' a mind to have a new beat - what will you sell me yourn for?"

"Sell my beat?" said Bet - "my beat, what mother bought for me? Not quite."

She turned on her heel, and walked down the street. At the corner, to her great annoyance and vexation, she met her father. He was quite sober, and came up to her at once and put his hand through her arm. His small eyes looked keenly into her face. When he was sober he was more or less afraid of Bet.

"So you give me the slip, my gel!" he said. "But I'm a bit too cute for that sort of game. You'd better tell me where you ha' put those two little boys of mine. They're my boys, not yourn, you may as well understand. Where have you them hiding, Bet? I'll find out; so you may as well tell me."

"I don't mind telling you, father. They're with Mother Bunch in Paradise Row - she have the care of them now. And, listen, father - they're going to stay there. Ef you want the boys, you must get round Mother Bunch first."

Granger's face grew purple. For some reason, this piece of information was most disconcerting to him.

"You're a wicked, ungrateful gel," he said. "You don't honor your parents - you don't respect 'em as has been put over you by Providence. You're a bad 'un, you are, Bet Granger; and you'll come to no good end. Them boys are mine, not yourn; and, for that matter, you are mine too - you ain't of age, you know."

"No, I'm not of age," said Bet, in a quiet voice. "But the boys are with Mother Bunch, and they'll stay there. Ef you really tries to get 'em away I ha' quite made up my mind what to do."

"And what's that, if I may be so bold as to ask?" inquired Granger, in a taunting voice.

"Father, there's people here - yes, here, in this great bad Liverpool - who help children when they are treated cruel. If you try to get at the boys I'll take 'em to the Refuge, and I can tell the people there one or two things about you what won't sound too nice."

This last frank statement on Bet's part was even more disagreeable to Granger than her first piece of news. He saw that his daughter was stronger and had a better case than he could possibly have given her credit for. This discovery did not, strange to say, increase his anger. His manner became quiet, and almost deferential.

"Look you here, Bet - what's the good of argufying, and angering a fellow what's your own father? You wouldn't stay in Paradise Row but for me - now, would you, Bet? It ain't the place a likely girl like you would fancy - is it, Bet?"

"I'm going to stay there," said Bet; "it's no question of like or not like. Mother Bunch's, Paradise Row, is where I'm to be found, ef I'm wanted."

"But look you here, my lass - suppose I was to promise you faithful that I'd never touch the lads - that I'd leave them with you to bring up as you could - suppose I was to promise that most solemn, and mean it most faithful; and suppose I was even to go from Liverpool - quite far away, say to London or some such place - would you stay in Paradise Row then, Bet?"

Bet looked steadily at the man who walked with slouching gait at her side. From head to foot she viewed him. Then she said, in a sad, deep tone:

"You're not likely to make that promise, father. Ef you did - ef you made it faithful and true, and ef you went away from Liverpool - why then, then I would not stay in a place what I hates."

Granger chuckled.

"I thought you were my lass, arter all," he said; "I thought as you was bone of my bone, and flesh of my flesh, and that you couldn't stand what's real awful low slums - *you*, as has been brought up in Sparrow Street. Why, it ain't likely - you, the neatest lass in the town - you, as I'm proud to call my daughter! Look you here, Bet; I'll give up the boys. Maybe I ain't fit for the sacred dooties of father. Maybe I am a bit rough, and a bit strong in my temper. I'll give up the boys, and you shall have them, same as if they was your own. I'll go away to Lunnon, and you shan't be fretted by the sight of your poor old father never no more, ef you make me a promise, like the good lass you are. We all know what Bet Granger's promise is worth, and ef you make it you'll keep it, Bet."

"Yes, father; certain sure ef I make it I'll keep it. What do you want me to say?"

"Why now - look you here, Bet; you'll never say again as your poor old father ain't mindful of you. I ha' got a mate for you, Bet - as fine a seafaring lad as ever stepped - always sure of his berth, and earning lots of money - a fine, honest, brave jack-tar; and he'll put you in a little place of your own, and he'll do for you and the boys, and I'll go away to Lunnon. There, Bet - the day you marries him, your father'll take third-class fare to Lunnon."

"Who is he?" said Bet. Her eyes shone, and the color flushed into her cheeks. Had Will Scarlett dared to go to her father. "Who is he?" she repeated - "but oh! it was mean of him when I said as it couldn't be!"

Granger, who was watching her face, laughed loudly.

"Ho-ho, my pretty lass," he said, you look very bright about the face for a girl what didn't care for a man. You take my advice, Bet, and don't send away your sweetheart: no young maid should do that. There - I needn't tell you his name when you know it. Come back with me now to Sparrow Street, and you shall see him, and we'll settle it all up, day and all, afore the night is over."

"I can't, father."

Bet's face had now grown deadly white.

"Will shouldn't ha' done it, for I give him my answer, and he knows I'm not the girl to change. I can't do that either to help myself or the boys, father. But what do you mean?" she added, suddenly, as a queer look on Granger's face caused her to stop. She wheeled round and confronted her father.

"You can't be asking me to go home to meet Will Scarlett; for he's away, miles away by now in the 'Good Queen Anne.'"

Granger burst into a loud, coarse laugh.

"Will Scarlett!" he repeated - "Will Scarlett? So that's the way the wind blows, pretty lass? But I look higher than that strip of a good-for-nought feller for you. It's Isaac Dent, the best seaman in Liverpool, as would wed you, Bet, and make you the luckiest girl in the place."

Bet put her hand to her forehead.

"Isaac Dent?" she repeated. "He drinks, he's cruel; he ain't even honest. Isaac Dent! Father, you must be mad."

She turned on her heel, and flew down a dark court, which happened to be near.

Granger called after her, but she neither heeded nor heard him. Like most cruel men, he was a coward. He dared not follow her into the place where she was seeking shelter.

CHAPTER X.

A few of the worst courts in Liverpool are absolutely without gaslight. It was into one of these now that Bet ventured. She leaned her back against the slimy, slippery, dirty wall, and breathed hard and fast. Her father could not see her nor find her there, and she was in a mood at that moment to fear no other living creature. Boys and men, girls and women, talked and swore and quarreled and jostled one another in the bad dark court. A lad of about twenty being pushed up against Bet, seized her familiarly by the arm; she flung him off like a young fury, and, wrapping her mother's plaid shawl which she wore about her shoulders over her head, ran out into the street. Her father was gone. Midnight was approaching, but the place was gayly lighted, for this was Saturday night, and the women, who could only get what was left of their husbands' earnings on their return from the public-houses, were eagerly buying and chaffering, and making what preparations they could for the coming Sabbath. No one molested or looked at Bet as she walked rapidly back to Paradise Row. She reached her destination about midnight, to find the whole house in what seemed to her the most awful state of uproar. Shouts and eager voices filled the air; loud laughter, screams of - "Hurrah! Well done! Do it again, Mother Bunch!" resounded on all sides. The door of Mother Bunch's apartment stood wide open; the small room was a blaze of gas and glowing from the heat of a great fire; and in the middle, with her arms a-kimbo, her head thrown back, and her bare feet twinkling merrily, stood Mother Bunch on a door, dancing, to the cheers of the audience, an Irish jig. As she danced, she sang; and it was to the tune of her merry voice and the movements of her rapidly-revolving feet that the crowd of spectators laughed and cheered.

"O, the shamrock, the shamrock, the green immortal shamrock - "

Mother Bunch sang these words with immense spirit, the Irish folks who looked on and applauded joining heartily and with vociferous cheers in the chorus. Bet had been dragged into the room, where she stood moodily, her shawl thrown off her head and lying in picturesque soft folds of color on her shoulders. Her handsome face attracted attention, and several people looked at her wonderingly; and one very rough looking man went up and addressed her.

Before Bet could reply, Mother Bunch had ceased dancing - had sprung off the dislodged door, which had been placed on the ground for her disposal.

"You leave this child alone, Dan Murphy; she isn't for the likes of you even to walk on the same side of the street with. Whoever says a word oncivil to this young girl shall have something to say also to Molly O'Flaherty. Now, out with yiz, neighbors all; the entertainment's over, and it's time for good folk to be in the land of dhrames. You stay ahint with me, Bet, darlint - I have a word for your private ear."

It was quite evident that in Paradise Row Mother

Bunch's smallest command was law; in an incredibly short space of time the little room was cleared, and Mrs. O'Flaherty and Bet were alone.

"Now, look you here, my love," said the Irishwoman, "you make what use you can of this yere arum," and she stretched out a most powerful, sinewy member for Bet's edification. "This arum shall come atween you and trouble, Bet Granger. You ask anybody round what they know of Mother Bunch, and a mimber such as this. You have no call to be fretted, honey, with this atween you and mischief. So go up to bed now; and swate dhrames to you, and the blessing of Molly O'Flaherty."

There was something so hearty in the voice, and so kindly in the gleam of the Irishwoman's twinkling eyes, that Bet's overwrought heart was strangely stirred. She stooped down and kissed Mother Bunch on her forehead.

"I trust you," she said; "you're a safeguard to me and the little lads."

And then she went upstairs.

Meanwhile, Granger, being much too cowardly to follow his daughter into what was known as one of the dark courts of Liverpool, shuffled back in a discomforted and savage mood to his own superior place of residence in Sparrow Street. There he found Dent awaiting him. Splendid jack-tar as he was, no one could be more thoroughly disagreeable than Isaac Dent when things, as he expressed it, "went agin' him." He did not care for his long wait in Granger's dreary, fireless room; and he cared still less for the remark with which Granger announced his return.

"It's all no go, Dent, my man. I told her what we said I'd tell her, and she went off in a mighty high tantrum. She's in Paradise Row with Mother Bunch - she and the lads; and I don't know how I'm to get them away from there. But," continued Granger, sinking into the first seat he could find, and stretching out his muddy boots, "you're about right on one point, old man - Will Scarlett's the lad of her choice, and not you. Why, she let it out as glib and innocent-like as gel could. Will Scarlett's the man, Dent; so you may put that in your pipe and smoke it."

Dent's ugly face grew a deep, dull red; his small eyes seemed to recede into his head, and grow deeper and more cunning. He did not speak at all for a moment or two, and when he did, the flush was succeeded by a more dangerous pallor.

"Look you yere, mate," he said - "you know a thing or two, and you has gone pals with me in a thing or two. It's nought to me who Bet cares about - she has got to be lawful wedded wife to me - or, or - you don't handle the coin, - you don't handle none of the coin, Granger. And you know a thing or two what would make it uncommon hot for you, if the wind was to blow in a certain quarter. You understand, and no words is needed. As to Will Scarlett, I checkmated him awhile back; so he don't trouble me. I'll say good-night, now, pal."

"Yes, but what's a fellow to do?" said Granger, in an extremely grumpy tone. "Bet's a strong lass, and a cute lass, and a cunning one; and she have got that Irishwoman Mother Bunch to back her up. I don't see what's to be done with a gel like Bet, if her will's fairly made up."

"I'd know what to do with her," grumbled Dent. He went as far as the door, then he turned suddenly - "Mother Bunch don't find her her bread-and-butter, I suppose?"

"No, no - Bet can do that for herself; she's a smart gel, and she have got the best newspaper beat in Liverpool"

"Oh, the best beat, have she? And she's your daughter - not of age yet - and she has carried the kids away from you - and she defies you, and laughs in your face? You couldn't think of a means of starving her out? Oh, no; not you! That good beat of hers - it were bought for her, weren't it?"

"Yes, years agone. Her Mother seed to that."

"Seems to me that as Bet's yourn her newspaper beat is yourn too. There's a tidy bit of money to be made out of such places once in a way; and there's such a thing as starving the wildest and sauciest lass in Liverpool into saying yea to your yea. A hint to the wise man is enough. I'll wish you good-night, mate. Only if I don't get the girl afore long, I takes the next berth that offers, and my money goes with me. Good-night to you, mate."

Dent went downstairs, and a moment after was making his way home to his lodgings. Bet had been perfectly right in speaking of this sailor as bad and cruel. Will was more than justified in any suspicions he might form against him. As Dent now walked through the streets his low type of face looked very bad indeed; the expression of cunning - that most unpleasant, that most diabolical of all expressions - was most apparent. It was past midnight now, and he cast sinister glances behind and around him. It would have been very unpleasant for him had certain people - Will Scarlett, for instance - the least idea he was still in Liverpool. Will, of course, supposed he was leagues away by now, snugly ensconced in that berth which he, Will, had been so loath to part with, on board the "Good Queen Anne." Will would indeed have opened his eyes had any one told him that Dent had never gone near the ship, and that the captain, after waiting and watching in vain for the bright young sailor whose name he had entered on his log, was obliged to choose another hand in a hurry, and knew nothing whatever of the able seaman whom Will now supposed was admirably filling his post.

For Dent had never the least intention of going away in the "Good Queen Anne." The one strongest desire of his life at present was to make handsome Bet Granger his wife; and he certainly did not wish to give Will a clear field in which he could woo and win her without danger or difficulty.

Dent had laid his own plans with care, and he was by no means depressed as to the possible result. When he reached his lodgings he lit a candle, and, first carefully locking the door, and looking round him with his most sinister glance, he lifted a loose board under his bed, and took from the recess beneath a sailor's checked pocket handkerchief. He opened it, and spread out on the table about twelve sovereigns in shining gold. "Six for me," he said, "and six for Granger, the day as Bet's mine. I ha' got a few shillings still, to hold out, and Bet must be mine by-and-bye. Six sovereigns to spend on

L. T. Meade

our honeymoon, and then to find another berth in another ship. But Will has got the notes. I might have made a better bargain with Will. Ten pounds is a deal of money to give away. But never mind - never mind: I have checkmated Will Scarlett with them notes."

CHAPTER XI.

A few days before the present date of this story a fair-haired young lady, with gentle, beautiful brown eyes, who was known in many of the Liverpool slums as Sister Mary, was going home late. She was dressed as a Sister, and belonged to a religious institution; but she lived with her own father and mother, in one of the great suburbs of the city. She was indefatigable in visiting the poor and suffering, going to their houses at all hours without a particle of fear, and coming scathless and without even an insulting word from many rough scenes and from many low haunts.

On this particular night she had seen to the dying Mrs. Granger's comforts, had said a word or two to Bet on her exit from the house, and then walked rapidly down Sparrow Street to the first tramcar which went in the direction of her home. A girl of her acquaintance got in also at the same moment, and the two sat side by side talking on subjects of mutual interest. The car was full; and a rough-looking sailor, of the lowest type of face, was crushed up close to Sister Mary. She sat with her back partly to him, and discoursed with eagerness to her companion. The sailor knew many tricks of sleight-of-hand - he was, in short, a kind of Jack-of-all-trades, and the laudable profession of the professional pickpocket was by no means beneath his notice. He managed to help himself to Sister Mary's purse without

L. T. Meade

her being at all aware of the fact. Her hands were clasped in her muff, which, though unprofessional, the cold night necessitated her wearing. She paid her tram fare with some loose change which she had slipped into her glove, and did not disturb the purse which she supposed to be lying snugly in an inside pocket.

Meanwhile Dent, for it was he, overheard some scraps of conversation of highly interesting nature.

Sister Mary Vallence had been at the bank that afternoon; she had been fortunate in getting to the Bank of England just before the hour of closing, and she described the race she had had, in an amusing manner, to her companion.

"Father would have been so put out if I had not brought him the money," she said. "He wanted it very particularly, for my brother Henry sails for America to-morrow."

"But are you not afraid of going down into these awful, awful slums with so much money in your pocket?" queried her girl friend.

"No, not really - no one would dream of supposing that I had close on 26 pounds in my inner pocket. As to the notes I always make a rule of taking the numbers. Well, good-night dear; I am glad I met you. By the way I saw that splendid-looking girl, Elizabeth Granger, again to-night I wish I could show her to you, Agnes. You would never rest until you had her for a model. Good-night, - I will get down here, conductor."

Dent also soon after left the tramcar; he had secured a richer prize than he had dared to hope for in any ordinary young lady's purse, and went on his way considerably elated, - only what a stupid, silly, almost wicked trick that was of people to take the numbers of bank-notes!

Miss Vallence went home, and very soon afterwards discovered her loss. It so happened that she had never noticed the sailor who sat next her, and consequently had not the smallest clue as to the time or the place where the purse was stolen. She had, indeed, never opened it since she had put the money given to her at the Bank of England into it, having enough small change for her immediate needs in the bag which she usually carried about with her. The purse had been stolen; but how, when, and where, were mysteries which no one seemed able to clear up.

The numbers of the missing notes were sent to the Bank, and a reward offered for the purse should anyone be honest enough to return it. The affair was also put into the hands of the police; but, as Sister Mary could give so little information, they told her that her chance of recovering the money was but slight. The only hope lay in the presentation of the 5 pound notes at the Bank of England; but even if they could trace the thing through this means, he was not very likely to change the notes at present. Sister Mary's brother had to go to sea without the money which would have considerably added to his comfort, and a bad man plotted and schemed to do much mischief through his ill-gotten wealth.

Bet was terribly startled when her father calmly and coolly proposed such a mate for her as Isaac Dent. During the first night she spent in Mother Bunch's attic, she lay awake and tossed wearily from side to side, trying to forget the evil face of the man who would if he could make her life, she knew, a hell on earth. She was glad of Mother Bunch's protection, and wondered if it would be possible for her and the boys to leave Liverpool altogether. But Bet, like most girls of her class, had an intense and almost passionate regard for her native place. The big town, with its wharves and quays and docks represented her world. She was at home in it; she knew both its byways and highways. To live away from the big ships and the rolling splendid river and the taste of the sea which was wafted to her sometimes on the strong fresh breeze, would have been death in life to the Liverpool girl. No; she would rather undergo any hardships in her native place than seek the troubles she knew not of elsewhere.

She reflected with satisfaction that her arm was strong as well as Mother Bunch's - that in her own young strength she could defy most dangers, and that these were not the times when girls could be forced to marry against their will.

Towards morning she fell into a heavy sleep, and awoke to find the boys both dressed after a fashion, and regarding her with round eyes of approval and satisfaction.

"I won my bet," shouted Thady, when his sister slowly opened her eyes. He began to turn somersaults in the wheel-like fashion which had drawn him sundry halfpence in the streets. "I won my bet," he repeated gleefully. "You'll have to give me the spotted marble, Nat."

Nat produced his treasure very unwillingly, and told

Bet upbraidingly that if she had slept one moment longer, so as to allow St. Jude's clock to strike nine, he might have retained his treasure.

"And you looked real beautiful with the fringes round your eyes as thick as thick," continued Thady, in an affectionate tone. "I'd have lost my bet jest to look on yer," he added.

"You musn't make bets about things, boys," admonished their sister. "Mother never held by betting, and you know, how I promised her that I would bring you two up. Now we'll light the fire and have a bit of breakfast, and then I'll take you to church. All good people go to church, I've heerd say."

"Oh, lor!" whispered Thady to Nat. "Arn't we going to turn out real pious!"

Nat was absorbed in the contemplation of his new boots, which he was now fastening on, and did not reply to his brother. Bet, however, shook her head; and the little captain, being oppressed by a sudden sense of perplexity over this new state of things, stood in a contemplative attitude under the skylight, looking up at the glimpse of blue sky and whistling.

The day passed in a somewhat dreary fashion. Bet took her boys to the nearest place of worship she could find - pushing them, in their decidedly ragged apparel, inside the church door, but remaining in the porch herself.

"You had better come in," whispered the verger.

"No, no; it's for them - get them the best places you

can," she said in reply.

And then she stood moodily just inside the porch, looking over the town, and clasping her hands with an excess of excited feeling now and then when the peal of the organ sounded on her ears. It was all beautiful and warm within, but she was outside. Was she to be outside everything all her life?

It is a fact much to be regretted, but both the general and the captain behaved so very badly inside the church, using their newly-shod feet with such vigor in kicking the boys next them, rolling their tongues into their cheeks, distorting their features, and finally exchanging marbles with their neighbors on each side of them, that the verger took them out before the sermon was over, and told Bet that unless she chose to accompany her brothers to church and sit with them during the service, they could not go at all.

"It's no go, Bet," said the captain; "we ain't the sort as you can make good 'uns of. Me and the general don't mind saying our prayers to you, Bet, and not turning head-over-heels in the street, and not betting of no bets, and we don't mind hiding if you tell us to hide, and we don't mind being locked up in the attic, 'cause it ain't 'ard to get on to the roof from the attic, and we can shy things at the cats from there: - but we can't set still in church - can we, General? No, never no more."

The General most heartily reciprocated these sentiments, and Bet perceived that it would not be wise to lay down the laws of supposed goodness too strictly in the case of two such adventurous spirits as animated the breasts of her small brothers. She took them for a walk in the afternoon, and it must be owned that the long day was dreary to all three, and that all felt oppressed with an unnatural sense of restraint. Nat, indeed, confided to his brother, as they lay side by side in bed that night, that he was afeard ef there was much more of that keeping in of a fellow he would have to go back to pie-crust promises, and do again what was pleasing in his own eyes.

Monday morning, however, restored a far less strained order of things. Bet was busy washing and mending, and doing all she could to put this new semblance of a home into order. The boys, delighted at not having to go to school as usual, whistled and cheered, and helped her to the best of their ability. In the afternoon she read them a very exciting story of adventure, which she had picked up in a penny paper, and again the little fellows assured her that there was no one in all the world like her, and that they would not hurt her, nor bring tears to her eyes, nor cause her heart to ache for all the world, - in short, that they would even be good for her sake.

"I'll find another school for you," said Bet, "what father won't know nothing of, and you shall go reg'lar from next Monday out. And now good-night, boys; I'll take the key of the door with me. See, I must have a good sale of papers to-night; for arter I have bought my store I'll only have tuppence left in my pocket."

CHAPTER XII.

Bet generally bought her papers at a tiny shop not far from her old home. She got them at wholesale price, and was well known to the woman who kept the shop. This person regarded Bet as one of her most constant customers, and now and then added a paper or two of the half-penny order to her bundle for nothing, and by way of good luck. On this night she informed her young customer that she had no copies of the *EveningStar* left.

"There's a run on it," she said. "There's news from the Soudan - something about General Gordon. Anyhow, it's sold out; so you had better take some more of the *News*."

Bet was vexed, for the *Evening Star* was the most popular of all her papers.

"I'm late to-night, and that's a fact," she said. "But you might ha' kept some of them for me."

"So I would, dear, but I thought you were leaving the newspaper business. A girl came in and said so, and she bought up all that were left of the *Evening Star*."

Bet was preparing to reply angrily to this when two or three ladies came into the shop who had to be attended to.

"I'd like to meet that girl," she said to herself as she walked rapidly to her destination. "What lies some folks do tell, to be sure!"

She was, as she said, late; and now as she walked along she opened her papers and sorted them, hoping that she had not lost many customers, and resolving that in future Nat and Thady should not hinder her from being in good time at her post. She was somewhat breathless when she reached it, and as she stood in the full blaze of the gaslight in her favorite position, her eyes were shining, and a rich color mantled in her cheeks. She looked positively lovely, and several people turned and stared at her. Her face was of a refined and even noble cast; and the incongruity of the uncovered head and the poor and tattered clothing only made her beauty the more striking. "Ha, ha!" laughed a coarse voice in her ear.

She turned quickly, - the dark, rough-looking girl who had accosted her on Saturday night was also standing in the blaze of gaslight; she also carried papers in her hands, and Bet saw that she held uppermost a great pile of the favorite *Evening Star*.

"Ha, ha!" she said, beginning to dance round her companion - "handsome Bet Granger! Lovely Bet Granger! But rosy cheeks won't do it, nor eyes that sparkle, nor lips that smile ever so sweet, when the beat's mine! mine! mine! Want an *Evening Star*, sir? Great news of Gordon in the Soudan! Great news from the Soudan! Soudan! *Evening Star!* Latest particulars! Fifth edition! Only a halfpenny, sir! Want an *Evening Star*, sir?"

"I think this is the girl who always serves me," said the gentleman now addressed.

He turned to Bet, and asked her for a copy of the paper.

"I have only got the *Evening News,*" she replied, in a dull, lifeless voice.

"Then I will take that," he said kindly.

He paid Bet the halfpenny, and went into his club.

"You had no right to do that, my pretty dear," said the dark girl. "I paid fifteen shillin' for your beat only this morning. I said as I were willing to buy, and your father he come and axed me, and I give him the money. What's the matter, Bet? You needn't look like that. Fair play's fair play, and the beat's mine now - I paid for it. You ain't of age," she added with a taunting laugh, "and your father had a right to sell, and the beat's mine now."

"Maybe you are telling me a lie," said Bet, still in that queer dull voice. "Some people don't mind telling lies, and you're one of them. I intend to go on selling papers here until you can prove as the beat's yourn." "Bless your heart, I can do that now - here. I suppose you know your own father's writing? See, there's light enough under the gas for you to read. There - see for yourself what he have said."

The black-eyed girl held up a dirty piece of paper for Bet's inspection. Like a flash she took in the meaning of the few words scribbled on it.

"This is to certify that I has sold the newspaper beat of my daughter, Elizabeth Granger, to Louisa Marks for the sum of fifteen shillings. - JAMES GRANGER."

"It's all right," said Louisa, as Bet handed her back the paper. "You haven't a word to say again it, have you?"

"No," said Bet, raising her voice a very little - "not to you. I haven't a word to say to you though you have stabbed me in the dark. I could fight you, but I won't; for you're of the cowardly sort that think nothing of lies, and creeping into a thing by the back door. You ain't worth fighting. I wouldn't have it said I touched your sort. Keep the beat that wasn't my father's to sell, nor yours to buy. Keep it; make what you can of it. Good-night."

The sparkle had not left her eyes, and the flush of exercise had given place to the flush of burning rage on her cheeks. She felt that she could have done that dark, malicious, talking girl an injury - only she wasn't worth it; she would pour the full vials of her wrath on other heads.

She walked away rapidly, not caring in the least where she wandered. At that moment it was nothing at all to her that she was ruined - that her means of livelihood had been snatched from her - that she had a bundle of unsold papers under her arm, and only twopence in her pocket, - that two little boys would be hungry to-morrow for the bread which she could not give them. All the pain of these things would come later to her; but just now she only felt her swelling, raging anger, and her burning thirst to revenge herself on the cruel man who called himself her father.

L. T. Meade

As a matter of course, she wandered into the slums and low places of the town - she eschewed the lighted thoroughfares, and walked along the darker streets. Her beauty was so remarkable to-night, that even here she was observed and commented upon; and with an instinctive, almost unconscious movement - for her passion absorbed her so much that she did not see the gaze of the passers-by - she raised her mother's worn, many-colored plaid shawl over her head, and partly hid her flushed, dazzling face in its folds.

Suddenly, in the midst of her rapid, headlong walk, she drew up short, pressing her hand to her heart, her lips parted, her eyes distended to their widest. She was listening to a sound, and that sound was saving her. The full, rich, delicious notes of a woman's voice were floating out through one of the dark courts to Bet's ears - the notes warbled like a bird's, they rose and fell like the clear cool sound of a fountain. Bet's great eyes grew soft - she knew the voice, and the music drew her as certainly as a troubled child will fly to its mother. She went straight into the court, and joined the group of listeners who were hanging on to Hester Wright's melodious utterances.

This special court was not lit by any gaslight, but a man had brought a rude, ill-contrived lantern, and by its dim, flickering rays the slight form and thin earnest face of the singer could be fitfully seen. A great crowd had gathered round her, but she herself was raised above the people by standing on a chair which one of the neighbors had fetched. By her side stood Will Scarlett. He joined her in the choruses, his voice answering note by note to hers; his face, too, was seen in the dim light, and Bet gave a start when she recognized it , and crept herself a little farther into the shade.

The wretched little court was almost full of people, fresh numbers coming in, moment by moment, as the beauty of the voice attracted them. These people belonged to the lowest refuse of Liverpool life; but they were all quiet, subdued, orderly - tamed, in short, for the time, by the magical gift which Hester possessed.

As a rule she chose grave music - it suited the depth and quality of her voice; but very rarely would she favor her audience with rollicking sea-songs, or anything with a comic element. Her taste, as regarded music, was absolutely pure and good, and she had a wonderful faculty for picking up both words and music of the nobler sort.

When Bet entered the court Hester and Will were singing "Kathleen Mavourneen." The fine range of Hester's voice enabled her to do this somewhat difficult melody full justice. Will helped her with a note or two now and then, for his own taste in music was nearly as good as hers, and he knew exactly when and how to aid without spoiling the effect. As each song was finished the people cheered, but not noisily; the cry was generally, "Give us more - give us another, Hester Wright!"

"Yes, I will give you another," said Hester, when "Kathleen Mavourneen" had come to an end. "I will give you something very beautiful now. I don't think you know it - it will touch you."

Her voice rose again into the air -

"I had a message to send her,
To her whom my soul loved best;
But I had my task to finish,
And she had gone home to rest."

All through the difficult evolutions of the melody
Hester's voice rose and fell; she rendered no note of the
music wrong; her unerring instinct and her real genius
carrying her through the most complicated and pathetic
music she had ever attempted. The breathless silence
grew denser, the people pressed closer, and Bet,
forgetting everything in the ecstasy of listening, found
herself almost pushed to the front: -

"And at last I know that my message
Has passed through the golden gate,
And my heart is no longer restless,
And I am content to wait."

"That is beautiful," said the singer. "Yes, those words
stir my heart - there's nought like music - no, there's
nought like music in all the world. Now, I'll give you
one more good thing - perhaps a better thing than that -
afore I go home. I heard it sung to the organ, and it
come from the inside of a church. I don't hold by no
church, but this thing has fastened on my heart, and I'll
give it to you, neighbors."

Hester stooped down and said a word or two to Will
Scarlett.

"Help me with the words, cousin - sing 'em out full,
and as if somehow you held on to them."

Will nodded, and the two voices, in perfect harmony,
once more filled the court.

"Oh, rest in the Lord. Wait patiently - patiently-for Him; and He shall give thee thy heart's - thy heart's desire."

As the last notes fell upon the listening people they might have noticed, had they not been so absorbed in watching Hester, that the man's deep voice shook and swayed a little. The fact was this: the flickering rays of the lantern had shown him the ruddy glow of a certain stately head, and for an instant a face shone out, and was lost again in the thick darkness. When the last notes died away Bet turned, and, pressing through the crowd, left the court; but the unerring instinct of love made Will Scarlett hear her departing footsteps over and above all the others. He said two hasty words to Hester, and followed her.

L. T. Meade

CHAPTER XIII.

"Bet," said Will, when they got outside; "Bet, I'm here. What is it? You're in trouble. I can tell by the way you turn your head away as you're in sore trouble. Why, there - you're sobbing. Don't, don't. It hurts me sore to see you thus."

"It were the music," said Bet. "Hester allays moves me, and there were words as brought mother back. I didn't hold to mother so much when she were living - I weren't never too good to her; but now it seem to me as if I fair hungered for her, and I'd like well to send her a message - many messages. Then, there were them last words. Why, Will, any one 'ud suppose that Hester were of mother's thinking. I never could have guessed it."

"Maybe she is, and maybe she isn't" said Will. "Seems to me the words is true, whoever holds on to 'em."

They were walking rapidly, and now Bet felt a sweet and yet rough breeze on her cheeks. They were down by the Mersey, and the salt taste from the sea was blown into her hot eyes and burning cheeks.

"That's good," she said, flinging back her shawl, and sighing, as if a great burden had been lifted from her. The moon was up, and its white light lay on the rippling water, and just touched the outline of Bet's face.

"That's good," she repeated, as she took another draught of the sweet, pure, invigorating air. She had again that pre-occupied look which seemed only half-conscious of her companion.

"Let's walk along by the quays," said Will. "Higher up it will blow real fresh; this is nought - only the shadow of the sort of thing that comes to you when you are fairly out on the waves."

"Will," said Bet, suddenly, as she turned and looked full at him, "I were fair wrapt up in myself, and it never come to me till this minute to ask how you are here. Why, it's nigh upon a week since you were to have been away in that ship that carried Hope at its bows, you mind."

"That's true," said Will, rather shortly. "But I had a wish to stay on shore a bit longer, so I sold my berth to Isaac Dent. He says he knows you, Bet - but he oughtn't to - he ain't fit for you to speak to."

"He's one of father's mates," said Bet. "And he's not at sea, Will; he's on shore. Father wanted me to come home on Saturday night last to see him, and to - to - oh, don't ask me - what father says has burnt into my heart, I'm wild to-night, Will. I'm wild, and tossed with misery, and that's the truth. Let me go home, Will Scarlett - that is, to what home I have. Don't, don't be clutching hold of my hand. I ain't fit to talk to a good lad like you to-night"

"Yes, you are, Bet," said Will. "You're more fit to talk

to me than to any other lad - or lass, for that matter - in the whole o' Liverpool; for I'm your true love, Bet, and you are mine. There - you can't go for to deny it."

Will's figure no longer looked so slight and boyish; he held himself up very erect, and the breeze tossed back his thick dark curly hair, and the moonlight shone into his honest blue eyes, as they looked straight at the trembling, troubled, excited girl.

"You know as I'm your true love; and I'll wed you, come what may," said Will Scarlett. "There - I stayed away from the bonny waves on purpose. Look at me, Bet, I'm the lad as has given his whole heart to you."

"I'm in sore trouble," sobbed Bet. "Will, Will, don't tempt me. I'm in the sorest trouble, and I'm being treated bitter cruel, and you - I know as you're honest - and I know as you - you could love a girl, and she might - might lean on you, Will. But don't tempt me, for I oughtn't to listen to such words as you ha' spoke. For I ha' made a promise as I'll never be wife to no man."

"You made a bad promise, then," said Will. "Who did you make it to? Ef it were to yourself, I don't see as you need hold to it, ef your mind's changed. And ef you made it to God, somehow I don't think He liked it, nor thought it a good word to pass your lips - for He have made you and me for each other, Bet; and I fancy as it don't please Him to have the plans as He has made crossed by the weak promise of a girl. You had better unmake that vow of yours, Bet; for it don't hold water nohow."

Will had now put his arm round Bet's waist, and his

eager masterful face was close to hers. She felt a new timidity, and a new trembling, wonderful joy stealing over her, and chasing away the dark cloud of her grief.

"I never thought as we was made for one another," she said, in a timid undertone.

"Then you knowed very little, Bet, ef you didn't find that out. Away on the sea, haven't I dreamt of you, and seen your face near mine, when the waves was rough, and we thought we'd be in Davy Jones' locker by the morning? And sometimes, Bet, when I'd be tempted to do as other fellows, and take to bad ways, your face 'ud come before me, and somehow I couldn't. I always knew when I was out on the waves that you was to be my lawful wedded wife one day. You can't go agin a thing like that, my dear. Why, when you come to think of it, it seems downright wrong even to name a promise you made only to yourself when you knowed no better."

"But Will - Will - mother was wed, and she suffered - oh, she did suffer bitter - and it were then I vowed as no man should call me mate."

Will's face grew dark.

"And you was right," he said. "You was mor'n right - when you thought of sich as your father, and sich as Dent. Why, Bet, sich fellers as them ain't men at all - they ain't worthy of the name. I don't want to say much, Bet; but I ain't of their sort - I could be tender to you, my dear, and true, true as steel; and your father couldn't touch you when you was my lawful wife, darling. And you should have the little lads, and keep the promises you made to your mother. See, Bet, the moon's shining on us, and there's a beautiful salt taste of the sea on our lips, and there's all the love that I can give you shining out of my eyes this yer minute. You make me a promise, Bet, dear - one that will undo that base one you once vowed to yourself. Forget that promise - what were cruel and wicked, and a shame, when it came atween you and me. Here, make another now, Bet - one of your own as never got broke."

"What shall I say, Will? I'm troubled sore, and yet I'm comforted beyond words to say; and you ha' done it! Will, dear Will. What promise shall I make as'll be true and binding on me forever?"

"Say this, Bet: 'I give myself to you, Will Scarlett, and I'll be your wedded wife as soon as ever parson can be found to tie us together. So help me, God Almighty.'"

Bet said the words without faltering, and as she did so a curious and wonderful thing happened to her - when she found her love, and believed in him, and gave herself up to him utterly, she also ceased to doubt that there was a God. He was there - He was good; He was blessing her. She had only twopence in her pocket, and her worldly career seemed a short hour ago utterly destroyed and done for; but now no girl in Liverpool could feel richer than she did.

CHAPTER XIV.

With people in Bet Granger's class the time between the wooing and the wedding is seldom long. Will would not go to sea until Bet was his wife, and so it was decided by the two that they would go to church as soon as ever the parson could be found who would be willing, as they expressed it, to tie the knot between them. Certain preliminaries had to be gone through, of which they were profoundly ignorant; and Will discovered, when he made inquiries, that a short delay was, after all, inevitable.

In some way, girls in Bet's class look upon marriage more solemnly than those who are born in higher grades. To them the marriage itself is all in all, - they have neither time nor money to give to dress and presents, and wedding paraphernalia. Bet would go to Will Scarlett in her poor, neatly-mended gown and when she gave herself to him she would bring him nothing else,-no outward adornings, no household furniture - nothing but just her steadfast spirit, her heart filled to overflowing with the greatest love she had ever known, and her great beauty. Will and Bet would have to live from hand to mouth, and would be still quite regarded as the poorest of the people; but love on such an occasion as this is very apt to laugh at poverty, and these two during the few days that followed were perhaps the happiest pair in the

L. T. Meade

great city.

As was to be expected, Bet had confided to Will and to Hester the whole story of Dent's proposal, and of her father having sold away her beat, and so deprived her of the means of earning bread for herself and her little brothers. Will and Hester between them had provided her with a little money for present necessaries, and Will told her that on the day they were married he meant to buy another newspaper beat for her.

"When I'm at sea you must be earning something, Bet," he said; "and though every girl can't hold her own and be good and respectable as you are, yet there ain't no fear for one like you, and you may as well go on selling newspapers to the gentlemen, and show them what a Liverpool lass can be when she likes."

"But the best beat is gone," said Bet, mournfully - "there ain't another to be had for love or money like that what mother bought for me round by the clubs."

Will's disposition was very sanguine.

"We'll find a beat nearly as good," he said in a confident voice. "There's a great club being built at the far end of Castle Street, and there'll be a lot of gas and light about, and the gentlemen will want their papers. I can buy a boat for you there for ten shillings, Bet, and you can earn a tidy penny. What with that, and what I can send you from sea, you and the lads won't fare so bad."

Bet smiled at these words, and was somewhat comforted - she had no idea of being a burden on the man who was to be her mate, and in particular was determined to support Nat and Thady entirely by her own exertions.

After a great deal of consultation, it was decided that during Will's first voyage after their wedding Bet was to remain in Paradise Row with Mother Bunch. This worthy Irishwoman took an enormous fancy to Will, clapping him on the back, cheering him on with his wooing, and assuring him that that "purty darling blossom of a wife of his" should be her first care, day and night, all the time the waves were washing under him; "and not a hair of her head should be hurt," said Mother Bunch - "and them mischeevous little varmints of hers shall come to no harm, naythur, - oh, will ye then, ye rogues! Why then 'tis you that bates the heart out of Molly O'Flaherty entirely."

With that she gave chase to the captain and general, who were dodging round the corner, and making anything but polite faces at her.

It is a very trite proverb, and a sadly worn truth, exemplified over and over again at all times and seasons, and in all places of the earth, that the course of true love never ran smooth; and alas! Notwithstanding all the pleasant preparations being made for them, these two poor lovers were no exception to the rule.

Bet and Will both had enemies, and these enemies were neither inactive nor inclined to forbear from mischief.

On the very day after her engagement Bet came across her father - she came upon him suddenly, and as if by accident; but in truth he had been looking out for her, as he was intensely curious to know how the starving process suggested by Dent was answering, and how soon, in consequence, he might hope to receive Dent's promised gold. No one knew better than Granger the depressing effects of starvation; he had gone through them himself, and was therefore an excellent judge. He expected to see Bet with her hair untidy, her eyes red and dull, and her face heavy, - he expected to be greeted with a torrent of withering anger and sarcasm, or to be assailed by a burst of violent woman's tears and reproaches. Instead of this state of things he saw coming to meet him a trim lass, dressed with remarkable neatness - her hair in a great shining coronet on her head, her eyes bright and yet soft, and a happy smile playing about her lips. Her face changed when she saw him, but it did not get angry, only a little pale, and the eyes took an expression of sadness.

"It weren't worth your while father?' she said. It were a mean, mean trick to play. It were a stab in the dark, father, and it took my breath away for a time, and I were mad with ye. Yes, Father - I was 'most quite mad in earnest; and ef I had met you last night, maybe I'd ha' done you an injury. I can't rightly say, only that I know that my brain was going round, and I was fairly choking with rage - it was as if you had put a devil into me, father."

"That's a nice way to speak to your own father, what give you your being," said Granger, in a puzzled, would-be indignant voice, for he could not understand Bet's speaking of all her trouble and rage in the past tense. "What's come to you, lass?" he continued. You was in a rage - ain't you in a rage still? - the beat's gone for aye and aye, you knows."

"No, I ain't in a rage now," said Bet. "It's over - seems as if there was a spring day in my heart, and I ha' no room to be in a rage. You meant it for bitter bad, father, but maybe 'twas God. I do think as it must have been Him - He meant it all contrariwise, and just because you sold my beat, as I were burning and mad with rage - I - I - never mind that part - only I'm the happiest lass in the whole of Liverpool to-day."

"You air," said Granger with a great oath. "It's like your impidence to defy me more and more. What do you mean by words such as them, you bad disobedient girl? Don't you know as there's a curse on them as don't obey their parents?"

"No, father; there's no curse on a girl who won't go your way; and though it ain't nothing to you, and I ain't nothing to you, yet I may as well tell you that I give myself to Will Scarlett last night, and I'm going to be his lawful wedded wife as soon as ever the law can tie us up."

With that Bet turned on her heel, and walked rapidly away. She had said her say, and did not want to listen to any of Granger's ill-timed comments.

Her quick steps soon took her out of the man's sight; he ground his teeth, and, choking with rage, went to find Dent.

"I could prevent it," he said, as he concluded his story. "The gel's not of age, so I could put my spoke in, and make it rare and troublesome for her. I will, too, ef you'll only put me up to the straight tip, Dent."

To Granger's surprise, Dent took all this information

with wonderful equanimity.

"I wouldn't try that on," he said. "Scarlett's of age, if the gel ain't, and you'd have to make a deal of statements, and maybe more 'ud come out than you'd like, and you mightn't gain your point in the end, for there's lots of ways of being married, and once the knot was tied you couldn't do nothing."

"You takes it mighty cool for one who wants the gel yourself," said Granger, who felt ready to dance with vexation.

"Bless yer 'art," said Dent, "you don't suppose as I mean to give her up? Not a bit of it. You keep yourself cool, old man; we'll divide the money, and I'll have my pretty bride yet. Why, Granger, you can never see beyond the stone wall you're gazing at; you haven't, so to speak, no perception at all. Now this don't surprise me, and I'll tell you why. I knew that Will wanted the gel - ay, and haven't I played him a trick on that very account? - and anyone could see with half an eye that she wanted him; and what more like than that they should make it up atween them. Yes, but wooing ain't wedding, and there's many a slip - oh, yes, many and many. Don't you fret, Granger - didn't I tell you as I had checkmated that low fellow, Scarlett? You won't never be demeaned by that marriage, my man."

With these words Dent left his companion; he had managed to comfort him a good deal, and he was certainly by no means depressed himself.

"Nothing could please me better," he muttered. "The thing's moving at last. Yes, my pretty Bet - you'll know what to think of that fine lover of yourn by-and-bye;

you'll say to yourself then that there are worse men in the world than honest Isaac Dent."

Here Dent laughed immoderately - the idea of taking up the *role* of an honest man seemed to tickle his humor to a remarkable extent.

"I mustn't leave a stone unturned, all the same," he continued; and after meditating deeply for a moment he strode rapidly away in the direction of the Eastern Docks. Here he entered a small shop, whose owner specially laid himself out to supply all kinds of heterogeneous things to sailors. There was scarcely anything that a sailor could possibly require which Higgins, the owner of this small shop, could not furnish him with. From wedding-rings to second-hand slop clothes he was up to all emergencies. There was no other shop exactly like Higgins' near this particular part of the docks; and because he was obliging in the matter of credit, and had a very jovial, free-and-easy manner, he was immensely popular with all the sailors who came that way, and in consequence did a roaring trade. Dent knew Higgins well, and was perfectly aware that his virtue was not above contamination. Higgins had, in short, such a keen eye for profit that he thought very little of stepping over the boundary line of strict honesty to obtain it. When Dent entered the shop it was, as usual, full of customers, but presently these cleared off, and Dent and the owner could indulge in a little confidential talk. They spoke in low tones, and Higgins' assistant, strain his ears as he might, could not overhear a word of their conversation. Several customers came in from time to time and interrupted them; nevertheless, when Dent went away he felt abundantly satisfied that he was laying his little trap with consummate care. Did Higgins know a sailor of the name of Scarlett? Of course - did a lot of business with him; as honest a fellow as ever breathed. Honest - oh! Dent raised his eyebrows, and contrived by various innuendoes to convey a contrary impression to the astute Higgins. They talked a little longer. Suddenly Dent became intensely confidential.

"Look here, Higgins," he said, "a word to the wise is enough" - here he pressed that worthy's palm with the hard, delicious pressure which an accompanying crown-piece can bestow - "look here, Higgins, if Scarlett brings you any Bank of England notes to change, be sure you get him to put his full name and address on them." Emphatic head-shakes, profound winks, unutterable contortions, accompanied this piece of sound advice; and Dent left the shop, having conveyed the impression which he meant to convey - that Scarlett had stolen some Bank of England notes, and that Dent for a private motive of his own, which it did not behove Higgins to inquire into, wanted to get him into trouble about them.

CHAPTER XV.

Will Scarlett's wedding-day had very nearly come. This was Tuesday, and on the following Thursday he and Bet were to go to church together, and to be made man and wife. On the following Monday honest Will was to sail away on a long cruise to China, and his young wife might possibly not see him again for a couple of years.

Never mind that; they were both young and buoyant with hope just now - in short, Will felt his love so strong that he was sure it could bridge the whole distance from China to that dread attic in Paradise Row, and surround Bet's heart and life with a halo which would make all things endurable to her; and Bet's love was also so strong - for it was a way of hers when she gave her heart to give it absolutely - that she too was certain that the golden chain of affection would reach from Paradise Row to China, and that, though outwardly divided, she and her brave sailor-mate would in reality still be together.

"You look out for the moon, Bet," Will had said to her. "The bonny moon will be shining on you and on me jest at the same minute; and the stars too, for that matter. Why, when one comes to think of it, we'll have a crowd of things in common still, sweetheart, although we has got to say good bye for a time."

In short, these young folks were in paradise just now. They were as poor as poor could be, and not an individual who heard of their relations to each other would have envied them; but love, which very often fails to appear on the threshold of what the world considers a great match, was shedding quite a golden glory over these two at the present moment. In reality, therefore, Will and Bet were not poor.

They were to part on Monday, but between that parting and the present moment would come the short church ceremony, and the little honeymoon, which they had arranged to spend at Birkenhead. Mother Bunch was to take care of the boys during Bet's absence, and the girl's own small preparations were nearly made.

On Tuesday she sat down in her attic and thought how a few short days had worked a complete revolution in her life. She was excited and hopeful and happy, and nothing was further from her mind at that moment than a certain dreadful old proverb which declares that there is many a slip betwixt the cup and the lip. The boys were playing in the back court behind the house, and Bet, having tidied up her very humble apartment, until, literally, there was not a pin in the wrong place, had risen to go downstairs, when she heard a lumbering, rolling, and very heavy step ascending. There was no mistaking who was coming to pay her a visit - no one but Mother Bunch could so bang herself against the sides of the slimy wails, or cause the frail balustrade to creak and groan, as she lurched in turn against it; no one but Mother Bunch could so puff and pant and groan, and finally launch herself into Bet's attic like a dead weight, and sit down on the pallet bed, spreading out her broad hands on her knees, and puffing more than ever.

"Oh, glory! them stairs'll be the death of me. Give me a drop of water, for the love of heaven, Bet, my dear. Oh, then, 'tis me as is the good frind to you; but 'tis black mischief as they're brewing agin' you, honey, and no mistake."

Here Mother Bunch recovered her breath, and Having taken a sip or two of the water which Bet gave her in a cracked teacup, began to pour out her tale.

"Come close to me, honey," she said, "for it's thrue as walls has ears, and when them as means mischief is abroad you're never safe, come what may. But we'll spite them, see if we don't - we'll be even with them - you and me, and the sailor boy. Oh, ochone, ochone! - but it's, a black world entirely!"

"What have you heard, Mrs. O'Flaherty?" asked Bet. She was trembling now, for Mother Bunch's evident perturbation had infected her. "Tell me the whole story, Mrs. O'Flaherty - you bring my heart into my mouth when you look at me like that, and don't tell me what the real matter is."

"Treachery's the matter, darlint - and a mane, cowardly trick to ruin an honest man, and to give the handsomest girl in Liverpool to a villain. Oh, no - I don't know none too much, only a word dropped here and a word there - and Mother Bunch being what we call in ould Ireland mighty cute, and able to put two and two together. There's a trick to prevent you and Will being wed, Bet; and it's atween your father and that low sailor feller he was talking to - and I heard it in the 'Star and Garter' whin I went there for sixpennu'th of beer just now. They never set eyes on me, becase I'm frinds with the man at the bar, ye knows, and I just dropped down on a bit of a three-legged stool near him, and wan't seen at all, at all. Thin I heard them a contriving and making up their bits of plans, and something was to happen on Thursday as 'ud take our breath away, and the sailor would have his own way; and Will-oh, I couldn't catch what was to be done with Will; but for certain sure he wasn't to be no mate of yourn; and-and-the long and short of it is, honey, that there's black treachery to the fore."

"Let me go," said Bet.

She had been kneeling by Mother Bunch, and drinking in every word. Now she stood up, and taking her mother's plaid shawl, wrapped it round her head and shoulders.

"I'm going out," she said; "see to the boys, Mrs. O'Flaherty. I'll be back, maybe, by-and-bye. Maybe I won't."

"I thought you'd take things in the right spirit, dear," responded Mother Bunch, who showed no particular curiosity to learn Bet's present purpose.

Having delivered her soul, she felt no further anxiety with regard to the matter. Bet was a strong lass, who, when apprised of her danger, could fight her own battles. With the remark that "she would see to the little varmints," and not expect Bet back until she chose to come, she rolled herself downstairs; and Bet followed her quickly, and soon reached the street.

She walked fast; her heart was beating, and her head was in a whirl. All her latent fear and distrust of her father had risen in full force. As to Dent-for, of course, the sailor was Dent-she regarded him with a kind of sick horror. Could she outwit these two who were plotting against her and her lover?-was there time?

She made straight for the place where she thought it most likely she should find Will. He generally spent his evenings with Hester Wright. When she reached the lodgings a neighbor told her that Hester was out; but as she was about to descend the stairs, with a sickening feeling at her heart, Will's whistle, as he bounded up three steps at a time, fell like the most joyful music on her ears. She sprang to him and clasped her arms around his neck.

"Will-dear Will-I ha' come-we must be wed to-night, Will."

She was panting and trembling, and her words were only coherent by reason of the great stress and force with which she emphasized them. Will wondered if she had taken leave of her senses.

"Come into Hester's room, Bet," he said, tenderly. "Here, set down, darling; why, how terrible you do tremble!"

"Oh, Will, I'm mortal frightened. There's more bad than good in this yer world; and the bad's agin' us-and bad things and bad people have such a power of strength in them, Will-and they'll part us if we don't outwit them. Oh, Will, let us be made man and wife this blessed night."

"But we can't, Bet. I'd like to - it could never be a minute too soon for me - but the license ain't due to me afore to-morrow, and Thursday is fixed up at St. Giles'

L. T. Meade

Church for the parson to wed us. Thursday is not so *very* far off, sweetheart. Why, I expect it seems longer to me than to you, Bet, for I ha' loved you, as Jacob did Rachel, for many a long year. What's two days when you ha' waited years?" concluded Will, and he put his arm round Bet and tried to get her to rest her head on his shoulder.

She almost pushed his strong arm away.

"You don't understand," she said. "It's to-night or it's never - it's you and me to go away to-night in the darkness, and hide ourselves for a bit, and let the wicked do their worst - or it's you and me to be parted, Will, and me to be hungering for you, and you for me - allays and allays."

Here Bet related what Mother Bunch had told her - that there was a plot brewing, and how her father and Isaac Dent meant to ruin her and Will. She told her story with great excitement and emphasis - her eyes flashing, and the color coming and going in her cheeks. To her it was a terrible story, replete with all possibilities of parting and disaster. The terror of it had taken hold of her, and her teeth almost chattered as she gave emphasis to her words.

To her dismay, however, she saw that the tale itself made little impression on Will. He was much distressed at Bet's agitation, and did all in his power to soothe her; but he could not get himself to believe that Granger or Dent could possibly injure either of them. He had all an honest young fellow's sovereign contempt for these worthies, and he even gently laughed when Bet repeated her assurance that the deep plot they were hatching between them would succeed, and part her and Will forever.

"I ain't afeard," said Will, stoutly. "I don't believe in there being any plot, Bet. Mother Bunch has just had a bit of a dhrame, as she calls it, and she didn't hear half she thinks she heard. As to Granger and Dent, I know they don't love me, and they might do me a nasty turn, if they knew how. But then, they don't know how, Bet, darling; and I ain't going to hide and creep away in the darkness, not for no man. You're shook with trouble, poor Bet; but there ain't no fear - not the least in life; and we'll be wed on Thursday, sweetheart, and have a good time afterwards."

"Oh, Will, Will!" said Bet. Her lover's want of belief in her story seemed to her the crowning drop. She clasped her hands, and suddenly went down on her knees to him.

"Let us be wed to-night, Will!" she asked - "to save me from Isaac Dent, Will! Make me your true wife to-night, whether you believe the story or not!"

Here she cried and wept, and wrung her hands.

Will was dreadfully perturbed-he did not believe in any danger for himself, but he was distressed for Bet. He raised her gently from the floor.

"You know as I'd take you to my arms this minute, darling, ef it could be done," he said. "But it seems to me they hedge round a wedding with a sight of difficulties, and you must either eat your heart out waiting till the banns is called, or have a license. My license is due to-morrow, but not afore."

The idea, however, of the license was very dim to Bet.

"I thought the parson would say some words, and we might be man and wife," she said. "You could send him the license, whatever that means, by-and-bye, Will-but I'm *sure* the parson would say the good words over us to-night, and then we might go away together. There's a deal of things can be done, if one but tried; and you and me needn't have our hearts broke because we must wait for daylight to get that bit of paper. Oh, Will, let's go together and find the parson. Dear Will, darling, let's go at once!-let's ax him, leastways-and if he says nay, we'll abide by it. Let's go, Will, now, this very minute. Let's find the parson, and abide by his nay or his yea!"

Will, bewildered, agitated by Bet's suffering and despair, yielded a somewhat unwilling assent.

"But I must go to my lodgings first," he said. "For I ha' got some money to change. Ef the parson can be found, and ef he'll wait for his license until to-morrow, and say the good words over us to-night, Bet, why, we can cross to Birkenhead by the last boat this evening. But I'd a sight rather wait till Thursday," he added under his breath; "for it seems like running away when there's nought to run from."

CHAPTER XVI.

Will's objection to so sudden a marriage was overruled by Bet's fervor and impetuosity; she would not listen to his objections, but every time he opened his lips shut him up with the emphatic remark, "It's now or never, sweetheart; ef it ain't to-night, something tells me as I'll never be wed to you."

She accompanied Will to the door of his lodgings, and paced up and down the narrow little street, chafing and trembling with impatience, while he ran upstairs to fetch the bank-notes which he had not yet changed. He came down in a few minutes, having donned his best jack-tar suit, and holding out a pretty sealskin purse to Bet.

"Just you see here," he said - "I found this in my room; I can't make out how it came there. Ain't it fine? Look - ain't it wonderful how anything can be turned out so neat? "and he opened the purse, and showed the bright red leather lining; then clasped it again, and stroked the soft seal covering.

"I'd like to give it to you, Bet," he said, "ef I knew how I come by it. It were lying on the floor, and the clasps shone when I held up the candle. I must ask Mrs. Jobling, my landlady, if she knows who it belongs to. It ain't likely as she'd own such a bonny bit o' a thing;"

L. T. Meade

he fingered the purse admiringly, and then thrust it into one of his deep pockets.

"I'll give it to you if I can't find the owner, Bet," he said in conclusion. "I don't suppose you ever had anything so bonny."

Bet, however, was far too impatient and excited to be interested in the most beautiful purse that was ever made.

"Let it be now, Will," she said. "Most like it belongs to Mrs. Jobling - don't let's think of it now. Have you got the money in your pocket, Will, dear? And shall we go at once and find the parson?"

A flush came up into Will's bronzed cheeks.

"None so fast, sweetheart," he said. "What would you say to us going to be married and having never a ring to put on that finger o' yourn? I han't bought the ring yet - the wedding-ring, darling; but I ha' got money to buy it - ten pound; it does seem a sight of riches. Let's go down to Higgins' and change the notes, Bet. We can get the ring there." Bet did not object - she turned at once in the right direction, walking so fast that Will began to chaff her.

"You take my breath away," he said. "You forget that I've got sea-legs, and ain't a match for the land folks when they go at that pace."

"Oh, Will - if you could be in earnest!" said poor Bet. "I'm hurrying 'cause it's life or death to me. It gets late, and parson may be out - oh! a hundred things may happen - oh, if my heart didn't beat so hard!"

"Well, here we are, dear," said Will, and the two turned into the small close marine store presided over by Higgins.

That worthy came forward himself to meet the handsome couple who now stood at the other side of his grimy counter.

"Evenin'," he said. "What may I serve you with? Why, if it ain't Scarlett! I didn't know you at first, lad, and that's a fact. Evening young woman! Courting, eh?" he whispered in an aside to Scarlett.

"Oh, that's about done," said Will. "It's marrying we're after - could you fit this here young woman with a ring?" he added, and he took Bet's hand in his.

A tray of wedding rings was placed on the counter - they were all second-hand, and some of them much the worse for wear.

Will made his selection, choosing a fairly solid gold band. He slipped the ring into his pocket, smiled into Bet's anxious eyes, and taking out his bank-notes, spread them on the counter.

"You'll oblige me with change for these, Mr. Higgins?" he said. "See, it's a nice tidy little lot of money, ain't it? But it comes in handy; for a feller ain't wed every day of the week."

"It air a lot of money," said Higgins, in a contemplative tone. He took up the notes, and fingered them, feeling their texture and looking at the backs. "It *air* a tidy lot of money," he repeated, and he looked keenly into Will's honest face.

For all his bronzing the color would easily mount into this young sailor's cheeks-it did so now, and he spoke with a little offence.

"You're wondering how so much comes to the like of me," he said. "Well, it's easily answered. I sold my berth in the 'Good Queen Anne'-about the neatest boat in the docks, and the jolliest berth a feller ever had the luck to find-for this yer money. It comes in handy now as I'm about to be wed. But don't change it if you have no mind to, Mr. Tiggins. I can pass it in at the bank to-morrow morning."

At these words Bet turned deadly pale and gripped her companion's arm.

"No," she whispered hoarsely: "we must have the change to-night."

Higgins, who had been watching the pair, now spoke in that oily and seductive tone which had brought many excellent customers to his door.

"What do you take me for, Scarlett?" he said. "Ain't you, so to speak, an old friend, and one of the best customers as this yer house can wish to see? Of course I'll change the notes, man, and good luck to you and your lass there. Yes - of course I'll change the notes; but seeing as I'm poor, and the times is 'ard, you won't object to the usual percentage for obleeging a neighbor?"

"And what's that?" said Will. "I'm in a hurry," he added; "so I'll listen to anything in reason."

" I charge interest a shilling in the pound , " said

Higgins. "That'll be ten shillings on the two notes, and the ring seven-and-six - seventeen-and-six in total; that leaves nine pounds two-and-six-pence change - and here you air. Only," here Higgins produced pen and ink, "you'll obleege *me* by writing your name and where you lodges on the back of the notes."

"What's that for?" said Will, drawing back a step or two.

"Nothing, ef you don't want to do it," responded Higgins; " only I can't nohow change the notes without - it's a precaution I allus uses with regard to bank-notes, which sailors don't have every day in their pockets. No address, no change - you can please yourself."

"Oh, Will, do write," whispered Bet; and so urged, Will did dip his pen in the ink, and scrawled his name in a somewhat uncertain calligraphy on the back of each note. Mrs. Jobling's address was further added. He then received his change, and he and Bet hurried out of the shop.

"Sold!" whispered Higgins to himself; and an ugly grin appeared upon his face. "Now to send these notes up to the bank the first thing to-morrow, - and - and - well, I have no love for Isaac Dent, and Scarlett's the sort of feller as no one could dislike; but the times is 'ard and the worst of us must live."

Here Higgins rang a little bell. When his attendant answered the summons he told him that he was going out, but that if a sailor called Dent looked in, he was to be asked to wait.

Meanwhile Will and Bet were hurrying as fast as they could to that part of the town where St. Giles' Church was situated. The church was a landmark, and it was easy to find it; and not very difficult, either, to ascertain where Mr. Phillips, the hardworked curate, resided. Bet, who could read well, had decided that they would apply to the curate, not to the vicar.

"Mother knew a little about Mr. Phillips," she said; "and I see his name on the notice-board. He'll be maybe more willing to listen, for mother said he were poor, arter a fashion, himself."

The little house at which the two stopped was certainly humble-looking; and the parson's study, in which they presently found themselves, was poorly furnished, with a threadbare carpet, a sad dearth of books, and a very feeble semblance of a fire. The curate, a thin, gray-haired man, with a stoop, rose from his chair as the young couple came and stood before him. Will was feeling intensely sheepish and uncomfortable; but Bet, with the eagerness born of intense conviction, had no room for self-consciousness.

"Ef you please, sir," she said, flinging aside her mother's shawl, and speaking not only with her lips, but with her glowing cheeks and sparkling, lovely eyes-"ef you please, sir, this is Will Scarlett, and I'm-I'm Elizabeth Granger. Mother used to mind you when you preached, sir; and she often comed to your church when she was strong enough. We was to be wed at St. Giles', Will and me, come Thursday, parson." Here she paused and gasped; and her eyes grew full of tears.

"Yes," said Mr. Phillips, in a kind tone. "You and this young man-a sailor, I see-are to be married on

Thursday; yes, very good. And you will make him an honest, faithful wife, I hope. Can I do anything for you? Anything to help either of you? Marriage is an honorable estate, none more so."

The tears were still brimming over in Bet's eyes. She had got so far, but now the words she wanted to say stuck in her throat. She looked appealingly at Will, who instantly forgot himself, and came to her rescue. Taking her hand in his, he led her up to the curate's little study table.

"It's this way," he said-"Bet nor me, we don't know the rights of it; but we've a mind to be made man and wife to-night, ef you're willing, parson."

The curate opened his eyes, and was about to speak; but Bet interrupted him.

"Will says the truth," she exclaimed - "we want to be tied up with some of the words out of your book, parson; so that no one can untie us, and so as we'll be true mates to one another for ever and ever. For Will and me we loves one another, and I could-yes, I could be good ef I was Will's true wife. But there are them - there are them as wants to part us, and to ruin me, and to ruin him; and they'll do it, ef you don't wed us tonight, parson."

"And we don't want to cheat by it," continued Will; "for we know that Government must have its fees; and the license is ordered, and you shall have it to-morrow, parson, and here's thirty shillings to pay for it. It ain't no case of cheating-only the lass here she's skeered like, and it's right as she should have her way. Wed us to-night, ef you can, parson," continued Will, and he

L. T. Meade

laid a sovereign and a half-sovereign on the little study table.

"Kneel down, Will," said Bet. "He'll say the good words over us - I know he will, and we don't want to cheat. It's only as we mustn't be parted. Kneel down, Will."

"She knelt herself, and held out her hand to Will, who dropped at her side. Nothing could be more impressive than the little scene, nor the brief expectant silence which followed.

"God bless you, my children," said the curate - "God abundantly bless you" - and he laid one hand for an instant on Bet's head, and the other on Will's - "but" - here he paused, and seemed to swallow something, and the next words came out with difficulty: "I can't do what you wish. I would gladly if it were possible; but it is not. If I were to say the marriage service over you tonight, I should be breaking the laws of the Church and the laws of England. I won't ask you what your need is, but I am quite certain it is sore. I would give five pounds this moment to be able to pronounce you two man and wife before you leave this room. But it is impossible; the matter is not in my hands. Trust in God, and wait until Thursday."

Bet rose to her feet without a word. All the color had left her cheeks, and the sparkle her eyes; and the hand with which she tried to rearrange her mother's shawl about her shoulders trembled violently.

"Good-bye, parson," she said; and she did not lift her eyes as she turned away.

"Good-bye, sir," said Will sorrowfully, as he followed her into the street.

"Parson blessed us, darling," said Will, putting his arm round Bet's waist. "Kiss me, Bet. Thursday ain't long to wait."

CHAPTER XVII.

Bet went home, and all Wednesday she stayed indoors, taking little or no notice of her brothers, and never alluding to the subject of the wedding which was to take place the next morning. The boys, finding her intensely unsociable, devoted themselves to their own occupations, which were, after a fashion, absorbing enough. They discovered how to climb on to the roof of this very tall house, and the spice of danger which accompanied such a proceeding rendered it quite delightful to them. From the roof of Mother Bunch's house they could slide or crawl on to other roofs; and Bet knew very little of the amount of liberty they enjoyed on these dirty but airy pinnacles.

She heard their laughter as they scampered in and out of the attic to-day without paying much attention to it. She felt stupid and heavy, and the excitement she had undergone on the previous evening had in its recoil reduced her to a state of almost inertia.

The slow hours dragged themselves along, and Bet's wedding-day, the day when parson could make her and Will one - when, the license being there, and the necessary formalities gone through, they might really stand up in God's house and have the sacred knot tied between them forever - had arrived.

It was a dull, foggy morning, with a drizzling mist. No matter; it was their wedding-day, thought Will, and no one could be more cheerful than he as he donned his becoming sailor suit and brushed his curly hair, and made himself look as spruce and neat as any jack-tar in the land. Rain and mist were nothing to this son of the briny ocean, the sunshine was in his heart, and he could scarcely believe in the wonderful good fortune which was to give him the brightest, the dearest, the handsomest girl in the town.

"Wish me luck, Mrs. Jobling," he said, as he rushed downstairs and encountered his sour-faced landlady in the tiny entrance hall - "I'm to be wed this morning to Bet Granger, the finest and the best lass in Liverpool. You needn't keep the bedroom for me, Mrs. Jobling; for Bet and me, we are going to Birkenhead for our honeymoon, and on Monday I'm off on another cruise. By the way" - here Will suddenly remembered the pretty sealskin purse; he thrust his hand into his trousers pocket - "is this yourn?" he said, holding the dainty treasure out for his landlady to see.

"No, no," she said, backing a step or two; "I'd have no call to a pretty thinglike that - why, it *is* fine! Looks as if it belonged to a lady. However did you come by it, Will?"

"That's more than I can tell you, ma'am. It lay on the floor in my room two nights back, and I picked it up. Well, if it ain't yourn, and I can't find no owner, it'ull do as a wedding-present for Bet." He slipped the purse again into his pocket and made off.

Hester Wright had gone early to Paradise Row to fetch Bet, for she was to be her sole bridesmaid - in fact, the only friend who was to see her give herself to Will. Will had no best man. But what of that? His heart did feel light this morning, and the gay notes which he sang as he hurried along the streets had an undertone of thanksgiving running through them. He was glad the day had really arrived, and thought to himself how relieved his poor girl would be, and how he could laugh at the unreasonable fear which she had shown two nights ago. He had certainly never guessed that Bet was nervous; but she had shown the most unreasonable, the queerest terror when last they had met. Well, it was all right now, and he could prove to her how vain were her alarms.

The doors of the church were not yet opened when the little wedding party of three met. Bet's face was still pale, and her eyes had a tired, almost hunted expression. She came close to Will and took his hand, utterly regardless of the significant looks of the passers-by. The words and glances of the multitude were nothing to her at that moment. She was holding her true love's hand; and the minutes were flying, flying, and the danger that she dreaded must be even now on their heels.

"What ail's you, Bet?" whispered Will, tenderly. "I'm here, and the hour ha' come. In a minute or two now nought can sever us."

Bet did not speak. She clasped both her hands over Will's, and looked anxiously over her shoulder to right and left.

"Don't worry her," whispered Hester Wright. "She has a dread on her, and there's no argufying it away. After you are wed it will pass. Don't worry her with questions."

Will sighed, and a cold little cloud seemed to come between him and the sun of happiness in which he had been basking all the morning.

Just then there was a bustle and a little commotion. It was only the verger unlocking the church doors. A small crowd of people who scent out even the humblest wedding had already collected-mostly ragged people, shoeless and stockingless boys and girls, women who sold watercress, one or two loafers from the wharves. Will, Bet and Hester were just about to go into the church, when into the midst of this motley group a man neatly dressed in plain clothes stepped briskly. He came straight up to Scarlett.

"Is your name William Scarlett?" he said, "and do you live at Mrs. Jobling's, No. 10 Quay Street?"

"Yes," said Will, in surprise. "I'm a sailor, and my name's Will Scarlet. I have a bedroom at Mrs. Jobling's."

"Yes, just so," replied the man. "Oh, come now, young woman - I've a word to say to this party by himself. Just you let go your hand, young woman, if *you* please."

Bet seemed neither to hear nor to heed. Her disengaged arm was now flung over Will's shoulder, and the hand which clasped his felt, in its intense grip, as strong and firm as iron.

"I knew that it 'ud come," she whispered between her set lips.

Will looked down at her, and something in her terrible agitation infected him strangely. He felt hot and annoyed and angry-almost angry with Bet, for losing her presence of mind, very angry with the stranger for intercepting him thus with ridiculous, senseless questions.

"Parson's inside," he said, jerking his thumb in the direction of the church; "and her and me is waiting to be wed. Ef you have anything to say to me, mate, I'll hear it later on, after we is wed. - All the same I don't know you, nor what your business can be," he added.

"My business is plain enough, young man. You're wanted, and you must come with me. I've a warrant here to arrest you on the charge of stealing two five-pound notes - same being passed through the Bank of England yesterday, with your name and address on the back. You'd better come off quietly, for there's no help for it, and the less you say the better, for whatever you does say I warn you will be used against you. Come, young woman, - hands off! You'd better let parson know that his services won't be wanting today."

Bet's head was now lying on Will's breast; her wide-open eyes were fixed on his face. He stooped down and kissed her. He was very white himself, and felt rather dazed, but his anger was gone.

"I can't make it out, sweetheart," he whispered. "It's an ugly mistake, and to happen on our wedding morn. All the same it's nothing in life but a mistake, my dear; and I don't see, if there's a scrap of justice in England, how I can but be back with you by nightfall, darling. You and Hester had better search up Dent, for he's the man to clear me, and I heerd you say as he hadn't sailed in the 'Good Queen Anne.' Now I must go with this feller; but I'll come back to you and Hester soon, for in course I can tell how I got the notes. Here I am - at your service, sir."

Will himself placed Bet's hand in Hester's. She had not said a word nor sought to detain him; but when he turned the corner something seemed all of a sudden to stop in her heart; and the strong girl fainted in Hester's arms.

CHAPTER XVIII.

In this land of justice there is nothing more incomprehensible than the extraordinary weight and power of merely circumstantial evidence. Never was there a more honest young fellow than Will Scarlett. From his babyhood he had lived by the golden rule which does to others as we would be done by; he had never given false measure, nor false words, nor had he been guilty of false deeds; in the true sense of the word, he was a Christian, - very bright, and gay, and jolly, and a prime favorite both with his captain and mates whenever he sailed abroad.

Nevertheless, this young man who bore so excellent a character was brought up before the magistrates on the morning of his wedding-day, charged with having stolen two Bank of England notes. As Will was being hurried to the police station, he felt quite certain that five minutes' conversation would set the whole matter straight; and he even wondered if Mr. Phillips could be got to return to the church later in the day to marry him to Bet. Bet's white, despairing face haunted him; and he tried to shut it away from his thoughts, and to dwell on the delightful anticipation of soon setting all her fears to rest.

But when Will appeared before the magistrates, matters did not go quite so easily as he had imagined.

In the first place, he was not allowed to tell his own story; and in the next, the sealskin purse which was found on his person was in the most remarkable way brought to bear witness against him. For a young lady and her father appeared in the witness-box who both identified the purse as hers; and this young lady with the beautiful brown eyes looked very sorrowfully at Will, but also said with great clearness that it was in that purse certainly that the recovered notes had been placed by her, and it was most undoubtedly out of that purse that twenty-six pounds in notes and gold had been stolen.

Will's anxious face cleared a little when Higgins appeared; but to his amazement Higgins seemed to be altogether on the other side - spoke of Will's eagerness and of Bet's trepidation, and how they both seemed in a great hurry and anxious to be rid of the notes at any price, and how loth Will was to write his name and address on the back. In short, everything seemed to go quite against him: and the one longing the poor fellow had was for Dent to be found - for, of course, Dent could and would clear him.

Finally he was remanded for a week, until some tidings could be got of Dent; he spent that night in jail, with all hope of a speedy wedding-day vanishing into the dim distance. Whatever happened, he had lost his berth in the good ship which was to sail from the Mersey on the following Monday; - whatever happened, too, was not his character more or less stained from this contamination with the prison?

When Bet recovered from her faint, she went straight home, but Hester hastened to the police-court, to learn Will's fate. He saw her as he stood in the prisoner's

L. T. Meade

dock; and all that eyes could convey of sympathy, and belief, and longing to help, she gave him. When the magistrates uttered their judgment, and it was decided Will should spend the next week in the lock-up, Hester did push near enough to him to say -

"I'll take care of that lass of yours, cousin; and she and me, we won't leave a stone unturned to find the man what 'as wronged you."

Then Hester hastened off to Paradise Row, where she had first a long interview with Mother Bunch, and then found her way upstairs to Bet's room. Bet was seated on the side of her bed; her hair looked rough and untidy; her poor dress was no longer orderly; there was a flush of defiance on her cheeks, and a hard gleam in her eyes.

"Well, ha' they done for him?" she said. "I never believed much in goodness, and this day - well, this day's work ha' finished me. Don't talk to me of justice, nor mercy neither. What ha? they done with Will, Hetty? He's the only honest lad *I* ever came across, - and there - he's took up for thieving! Oh, don't ever talk to me about there being real goodness in the world."

"You talk silly," said Hester. "It's badness has ruined Will Scarlett. The bad heart of a real wicked man has spoiled the honest lad. Don't talk about what you know nought on, Bet, but think how we can serve him. He's locked up for a week, so that Dent may be found and brought to confess. You and me has a power to do in a week, and we have no time to talk silly words, what have neither sense nor meaning in 'em."

Bet's face changed while Hester was speaking. The defiant, almost repellant, look left it: it did not regain any of that strange softness which transfigured it when in Will's presence; but it was no longer hopeless; the idea of work to be done had driven away the cruel demon of despair.

"Oh, Hetty," said Bet, running up to Hester, and dragging her down to sit beside her on the pallet bed. "I'm glad as there's summut to be done. Mother allus said I was a hard 'un, and that the Almighty hadn't no love for such as me. And I did feel hard arter Will were took away - for I never had no real happiness, Hester, until arter Will and I promised to wed each other - and I thought it must be true about the Almighty hating such as me when He took Will from me at the very church door. But I don't mind anything now, Hetty, if there's ought as I can serve the lad with. I'm despert - I'm despert, as far as I think of myself, but there's nought - *nought* - as I wouldn't do to serve Will. I'd break a promise - I'd break a promise made to the dying, - me, who never broke my word! - ef it would serve the lad I loves. There, Hetty - no one can go further than that, - no one can speak more solemn and meaningful."

"Poor Bet!" said Hester. "Your heart's wrung, my dear - your words are wild, but their meaning's true enough. Will 'ull get a good wife in you, Bet, and you'll forget an evil day like this by-and-bye. But now," she added, "we has got to plan and to contrive, and the main thing is to find that villain Dent. I were at the police-court all day, and I heard every word, and it seemed to me them men could twist anything, and turn black into white, and t'other way, just as it pleased them. And they did say things agin' Will as most took

L. T. Meade

my own breath from me; and all the time the lad stood there, with his face as honest as the sky, only a bit puzzled like. But it seemed to me, and that's what I come to you for, Bet, that the only chance for our poor Will is to find that villain Dent, and get the truth out of him some way. You said, Bet, that Dent hadn't sailed in Will's ship - oh, it's plain to be seen as he give the lad the money just to get him into this trouble. And Will, he's like a baby, for thinking innocent of all the world. Well, well, I mustn't dwell on it, for my own heart burns; but ef you know where Dent is hiding, Bet, you might get news of him, and bring me word as quick as may be."

"I don't know where he hides," said Bet, "but all the same I might get news of him. I think I know a way," she added, her face growing white again and hard, - "you go home, Hetty; it ain't for you to help me again in this matter, - you know my mind, and how I wouldn't stop at nought when I'm torn as I am to-night. But it ain't for you to help me in this. You go home, Hetty dear; and ef I have news I'll look you up later on." "Then I'll take the lads with me," said Hester. "You can't do nought with them when you're all upset as you are now; and they'll be good with me, and I'll give them summut to eat. Why Bet, my dear, you needn't take it in that way; for if I didn't do a good turn to the poor little chaps for their sake and your own, wouldn't I do it for Will, as is my own cousin, and who I love better than anybody else in the world? Don't you take on now, dear - don't you," for Bet had flung her head down on her hands, and was giving way to the most terrible, heartbreaking sobs.

"Oh, the poor lads!" she said - "the poor, poor, little lads - and my promise tomother! But there-Will comes afore all. Take 'em home, Hetty, and give 'em the best you can for to-night. No, no, boys - don't come for to kiss me - I ain't a good sister to you no more."

The captain and the general paid no particular attention to Bet's manner. They were sorry she was in trouble, but the delight of going off with Hester soon made this dismal remembrance fade from their baby minds. The little party went away, and Bet was left alone in her attic.

Her bridal night! - but what a night! Will lying lonely and forsaken in his prison cell, and she - she, Bet Granger, the poor, but also the honest and upright, about to be unfaithful to the most solemn vow she had ever taken in her life Never mind; love must still be lord of all, and Will must be saved at any price.

She wrapped her shawl about her stately head, smoothed back the fuzzy red-gold locks, and went out into the desolate winter night. She left Paradise Row quickly behind her, and in a very short time was once more in Sparrow Street She stopped at the familiar door, and ran quickly up the stairs. Her heart almost choked her as she stood for a moment outside the door of the room where her mother had died. There was no sound; she turned the handle and went in. The room was empty, and looked untidy, dirty, desolate. A little fire, however, lingered in the grate, and a paraffin lamp smoked and smelt horribly on the dirty deal table. Bet tucked up her dress, and in a few moments transformed the room. The fire was built up, and burned brightly; the lamp was trimmed, the ashes were swept out of the grate, and the chairs were dusted and put tidy. She found a dirty cloth which ought to have been white, shook it and smoothed it out, and covered the deal table with it. She laid a couple of horn knives and forks, a couple of cracked plates, and a glass or two on the table. There was no food, however, in the cupboard, and she had no money in her pocket to buy any. She sat down now by the glowing fire, and waited. She had tossed off her shawl, and the firelight fell on her pale, proud face; her lips were very firmly set, and her resolute eyes looked into the fire. Inwardly she was faint and sick, for she had not tasted food that day; but she was unconscious of absolute hunger, all the energy within both soul and body being fixed on one idea.

A step was heard on the stairs - a shambling step. Bet knew it. She stood up, and when her father entered the room, confronted him with eyes that almost blazed.

"Here I am," she said. "I have come back - you can have your way. You didn't starve me out, but you took my heart and crushed it - you crushed it under your foot. You're a bad man; there's only one worse than you, and that's Isaac Dent. I have come back, and I'll stay ef you'll take me on my own terms. Not unless - mind you that - not unless."

Granger was a little the worse for drink. He was not really tipsy, but he had taken enough slightly to confuse his brain; and the altered aspect of the room and the sudden apparition of his daughter almost paralyzed him.

"Well, I never!" he exclaimed, and he sank down, an abject-looking figure, on the nearest chair.

"Do you hear me, father?" said Bet. She came up close and stood over him. "I ha' come back, Ef you give me my terms, I'll stay. I'll stay, and I don't mind owning that I've been conquered. I'll do for you, and tend you, and keep the place tidy for you, same as I did when mother was alive, and what money I earns you shall share. I'll be as true a daughter to you, father, as ef - as ef you was good. You want some one to cosset you up, don't you father? You give me my way, and I'll do it. Cosy will be no name for you, father, and snug no word for this yer room."

Here Bet knelt down, and laid her shapely hand on Granger's arm; her eyes looked into his, and her lips, so hard and firm a minute ago, absolutely smiled.

"You're none so young as you were," she continued; "you're getting on in years, and your step's a bit shaky, and your hairs are turning white. You wants your comforts, father - course you do. Why, this room - it was shameful when I come in, and look at it now! - it's a bit spry, ain't it now?"

"For sure, yes; it *is* spry," said Granger, glancing round him in a nervous, anxious manner.

His daughter's strange demeanor and unusual gentleness by no means reassured him.

"What are you arter, Bet?" he said, as gruffly as he could manage to speak. "You don't bring honeyed words like them 'ere into this house for nothing. Tell out what you wants, and don't talk flummery."

"I wants you and Dent to take the shame off Will Scarlett," said Bet. "There's no flummery there - that's my meaning, spoke out plain. You two ha' put shame on Will, and cast him into prison, and I want you to

L. T. Meade

take him out again, and lift the shameful lie off him. That's all - it ain't much, and it 'ull be the better for your souls - ef you have any souls - that you should do it."

Granger burst into a loud laugh.

"You have the cheek!" he said. "And for you to wed him, I suppose, the werry minute as he gets his liberty! No, no, Bet - none of that. I ain't much - for sure I ain't much; but a gel brought up in Sparrer Street shan't wed with no thief. There - I'm going out. I know nought about Will Scarlett. Neither Dent nor me could open his prison doors for him. You talk rubbish, Bet, and I'm 'shamed to hear you. I'm going out - you can set by the fire as long as you pleases, or you can go back to Paradise Row."

Granger turned to the door. But Bet was before him. She turned the key in the lock and put it in her pocket.

"No, no, father; you don't go out until you hear my terms," she said.

CHAPTER XIX.

All her softness had deserted her. She looked like what she was - a wild, untamed creature brought to bay.

"You ha' got to hear my terms, father," she said. "I'll be a good daughter to you, but I want Will out of prison. You don't suppose as I don't know what you and Isaac Dent ha' done to my Will. You was mad as I should be happy with Will, and Isaac Dent was mad 'cause I shouldn't mate with he; and Isaac Dent stole the five-pound notes and the purse, and other money besides, and he knew as the number of the notes was took, and he was frightened, and so he give the notes to Will, and pretended as he wanted to buy his berth in the 'Good Queen Anne.' But Dent didn't sail in that ship, father, and Dent's in Liverpool now - I know he is, for you axed me to meet him here some time back, and Mother Bunch seed you and a sailor lad in the Star and Garter this week, and she heerd you plotting and planning, and she knew - she guessed as there wor mischief brewing. There's a case agin' you and Dent, father, and you'd better come to my terms, or it 'ull fare worse with you. No harm'll come to you; but Dent - he must be found, and Will must be set free. There - you've got to do that; do you hear me?"

Granger crouched near the door. He neither liked Bet's manner nor her words. She knew a great deal more than he had the least idea of. Mother Bunch having overheard him and Dent as they laid their plans together in the Star and Garter was an awkward circumstance. The whole thing looked ugly. He wished he were out of it. More particularly as he had never received any of Dent's promised gold.

It behoved him, howe'er, to be careful, - on no account must he betray himself or his fears to this astute daughter.

"You needn't speak so loud, Bet - I ain't deaf. It's a queer world, - it's a nice state, so to speak, of society when a gel takes to bullying of her own father. You're quite mistook ef you suppose Dent is in Liverpool. A life on the ocean wave, with its storms and its fogs and its dangers, is poor Dent's life at present. But I don't say," continued Granger, lowering his voice, and trying to speak in a seductive manner, "I don't say as I couldn't get word with him. I won't say how, and I won't say when; and I won't say, either, but what he's as innocent as a babe; but word with him I might be able to get ef, - now, what's the matter, Bet?"

"Nothing, father - nothing much - only set you down by the fire and make yourself cosy. There - you're all trembling; you're not as strong as you ought for to be - you wants your comforts. You'd like a cup of tea now, wouldn't you? And no one can make tea like Bet - now, can they?"

"That's true enough, my gel - you can be a comfort ef you have a mind. No mistake on that point. Well, as I said, I might get word of Dent, - only hark you, Bet, you'll stay at home - there'll be no larks back to Paradise Row, and no bringing Mother Bunch to the front? You'll stay here, and be a comfort to your father?"

"Yes, father, I said I would, - oh, I can make you real cosy, there's no doubt on that point."

"And you'll bring the lads back, and not play no fool about them no more? They're my lads, and you has treated me shameful in the matter. But you'll bring 'em back, to be under the shelter of their honest father's roof? You understand - I'll do nought about finding Dent unless you comes back here - you and them boys." Bet's face was convulsed for a moment.

"They shall come back," she said, then - "that's the 'greement: me and them living here as of old, and Will let out of his prison."

"And there'll be no talk of your marrying yourself to the thief? I'll do nought ef you give me that feller as a son-in-law. I'd rather a sight leave him in prison - why, Bet, how white you air - I wouldn't be doing my dooty as a father ef I seed you a flinging of your 'andsome self away on a thief feller."

Granger was right when he said Bet's face had grown white. Her long fast, all the anguish and agitation she had undergone, and now this terrible last clause in the agreement she was making with her father, proved too much for her. She did not faint, as she had done in the morning; but she was absolutely incapable of replying. Her lips opened, it is true, but no articulate sound came from them.

"I'm a bit weak," she managed to gasp at last; "I han't eaten nought to-day."

Granger fetched her a little water, and then volunteered to go out to bring in bread and tea. He was still considerably puzzled and annoyed at Bet's knowledge of his doings; but he was glad to have the girl and the boys once more in his power, and had great faith in Dent's diplomacy.

Dent would soon settle things, and Bet should be his wife as quickly as the license could be purchased.

CHAPTER XX.

The police were searching everywhere for a sailor called Dent. They set detectives to work, and had little doubt that long before the week had expired for which Will had been remanded they would find their man, and establish the truth, or otherwise, of Will's story.

When it commenced it seemed quite an easy search; but the days flew quickly, and neither about the docks, nor loafing round the quays, could anyone least bearing Isaac Dent's description be found. His name was not on any ship's log, and the police came to the conclusion that Liverpool really did not contain him. They advertised - they even offered rewards for the slightest information; but no clue could they obtain. On the seventh day of Will's captivity they gave the matter up as a bad job, and said that the sailor Dent was not in the city.

They were mistaken. Dent had never left his native shores. He was not particular as to his quarters - he was clever at disguising himself; and as there are in Liverpool courts and slums into which no policeman cares to venture, it was not very difficult for Dent to elude these worthies.

Granger, however, had found him out, and Granger and he had many colloquies, but not in a place where

L. T. Meade

Mother Bunch could overhear.

"I ain't afeard," said Dent. "They can do nought to me, nor to you neither, mate. I'd like to go to the police court - and I will, too. But it won't be to clear Will - by no means, but quite the contrairy. Only I don't choose the police to be dragging of me forward. I'll go when I has made terms with Bet, and not afore."

Then the men whispered together again, and laid their plans, which were quite as deep, and quite as wicked, as the most unprincipled could desire.

Bet lived once more in Sparrow Street, earning thereby Mother Bunch's contempt, and a queer, puzzled look from Hester Wright, who would not forsake her, but who certainly failed to understand either her or her motive. She brought the boys home; and now her father's room in Sparrow Street was kept fairly neat, and the lads resumed the life which had been broken off at their mother's death. They shrank from their father, who, absorbed in other things, did not trouble them much just then; and they looked with great wonder and perplexity at Bet. She was not the Bet of old; she took scarcely any notice of them; she never smiled when they came near her; she said nothing at all now about their being good boys, and never by any chance did she allude to their mother's name before them.

She spent her whole time watching and listening, - starting and changing color at the merest sound, looking eagerly at her father whenever he came into the house, avoiding Hester Wright, eating next to nothing, wearing away her sleeping hours in long, exhausting fits of weeping. Will's week in prison was nearly over, and Bet in the time had changed - changed so much that it almost seemed as if years had gone over her head. Her cheeks were thin, all the color had left her face, and her eyes looked now too bright and large for beauty.

On the day previous to Will's again appearing before the magistrates the poor girl's restlessness became almost unbearable. Granger still gave her to understand that Dent was not in Liverpool. He would find him - yes, he said, he was certain to find him; but Bet did not know that he had done so, and her terrors were proportionately great. She could not sit still for a moment - but paced up and down, up and down the small room where her mother had died, like a caged animal.

The captain and the general were off on expeditions of their own; hours passed, but no one came near the unhappy girl.

At last, when her impatience had almost burst bounds, Granger arrived.

"I ha' done it, Bet," he said. "It rests with you now - Dent is found."

"Thank God!" she exclaimed, involuntarily. She fell on her knees before her father and clasped his hands. "Feel how my heart beats," she said - "I were nearly going mad. Father, there'll never be a better daughter to you than me in all Christendom, from this time out. You ha' found Isaac Dent, and he'll be in the witness-box to save Will to-morrow. Thank God Almighty! There's hope yet in the world."

"I ha' found Dent," continued Granger, rubbing his rough sleeves across his mouth in a furtive manner. "I told him about Will, and he's willing to go to the police-court to-morrow - that is, ef you're agreeable."

"I agreeable, father?" Bet laughed excitedly. "You know my mind on that; and so does Dent. Why, I could almost find it in my heart to call him a good feller, ef he saves my lad."

"Ay, Bet - that's just it." Granger shuffled again, and would not meet his daughter's eye. "He wants you to call him a good feller; he wants you to be werry particular kind to him, seeing as he won't stir hand nor foot to save Will Scarlett until you takes yer oath as you'd wed with him. Ay, that's it, Bet - you ha' got to face it; by no other means can you set that lad of yourn free. You ha' got to face it, and Dent must have his answer to-night."

Bet did not speak at all for about a minute.

"I feared as this might come," she said at last In a queer voice. "I did hope as God Almighty might have spared me. But it weren't to be. It's miles worse nor giving up my life."

She had been kneeling by her father; now she started to her feet, and wrapped the plaid shawl about her head and shoulders.

"I'm going to Hester," she said. "I'll give you your answer when I comes back."

CHAPTER XXI.

Bet walked quickly through the streets. She pushed back her hair under her plaid shawl: her eyes looked bright, and her step was once more firm and erect.

"There are all kinds of love," she kept muttering to herself - "all kinds-there's the love that gives, and the love that gets. Seems to me that mine must be the love that gives."

A queer little smile came over her face as this thought entered her brain. She walked still more quickly, and clenched her strong hand, while resolution and the noble determination of self-sacrifice gave her a false strength. Bet was not ignorant of certain verses of the Bible. She had never read the Bible, for her mother's form of religion had rendered the idea of looking into its pages distasteful to her; but words from it had been quoted many times in her poor home, and one of its verses now floated into her memory: *"Greater love hath no man than this - that a man lay down his life for his friend."* The words brought with them a healing sense of comfort. She really did not know from where they were taken, but she found herself repeating them, and she knew that if she really agreed to marry Dent, she would give up far more than her life for Will. No questionings as to the right or the wrong of this action came to perplex her - she never for an instant supposed

L. T. Meade

it possible that Will could prefer prison with the thought of her waiting for him at the end, to liberty with her lost to him forever. No, no; sailors, of all men, must be free - free as the wind or the air. Will must once more go where he pleased, and taste the briny ocean in salt spray on his lips. Confinement would kill a roving spirit like his. He would be sorry to have lost her - Bet; but by-and-bye he would find another lass to comfort him.

Just at present Bet had a sense of exaltation that caused her scarcely to feel any pain. The worst had now come and was over - her heart beat calmly; she had nothing further to dread; and she ran quickly up the stairs to Hester's room, and looked in with almost a bright face.

"I ha' come," she said, drawing her breath fast, - "Dent is found, Hetty, and Will will be free to-morrow night."

"Oh, how glad I am!" said Hester. She had been making up her fire and tidying the room before going to rest. She went straight up to Bet, now, and put one arm round her neck, and raised herself a little to kiss the taller girl.

"You'll be happy, yet, Bet," she said; "and God knows I'm glad of it." Bet did not respond to Hester's kiss. She held herself very erect, and looked down calmly into the singer's eager, enthusiastic face.

"It's a good thing Dent is found," she repeated. "I came to you Hetty, to ask you ef you'd help me to write a letter to Will. You're more of a scholard than I am, and I thought maybe atween us I might make my mind known to the lad."

"For sure, Bet, I'll help you to write," said Hester. "But ef Dent is found, and witnesses for Will, you'll see him in a few hours, honey; and it don't seem worth while to put into writing what can be told with the lips."

"I'll see Will to-morrow," repeated Bet, "for I'll be in the police-court; but, all the same, it's my mind to put a few words in writing, so that the lad may know clear what my meaning is. You'll help me, won't you, Hetty, seeing as you're more of a scholard than me?"

"To be sure I will," said Hester. And going to a drawer, she took out a penny bottle of ink, an old pen, and a sheet or two of very thin, poor writing paper.

"Shall I write or will you?" she said, looking up at the girl, who stood still and upright in the middle of the room.

"Set down, Bet, dear, and take the pen in your own fingers - ef the letter's for Will, he'd like to have the writing yours. Set down, and I'll help you to spell out the words."

"No," said Bet; "I ain't a scholard, and my hand shakes. I'll say what's in my heart, and you'll write it for me, Hetty, dear."

She moved over now to the fireplace, and leaned one elbow on the tiny mantel-shelf; her face was quiet, but Hester could not help remarking the absence of hope in her eyes.

"Are you sure that Dent will appear in the witness box?" she asked. "Seems to me as if he'd scarce dare to; for he'll have to say how he come by the notes. You

L. T. Meade

know, Bet, and so do I, that he's the real thief; and ef he appears to clear Will, seems to me he must confess his own share. Are you sure as he'll do it, Bet?"

"He told father so," replied Bet. "He's deep, and he'll find a way. He said as he'd do it for a price - it were a heavy one - he wouldn't do it for nought else; he named his price, and he promised that for that he'd clear Will."

"I don't see how he's to do it," repeated Hester, looking more and more dissatisfied. "Dent ain't the man to pop himself into the jail. And a price? You and Granger han't got any money. It's deceived you are, I fear me, Bet."

"No," said Bet - " the price is *me* - there ain't no deceit, and his meaning's quite plain. When Dent saves Will, he's to have me. I'm to wed him - them's the terms - there ain't no use argufying, Hester; but it's all plain - Dent will clear Will, and keep out of prison hisself, for he's as clever as he's bad. And I'm to be his wife. Now you write the letter."

"That I won't," said Hester, flinging down her pen. "Ef you think I'm going to break Will's heart, and yourn, too, you're fine and mistook. Dent is playing the fool on you, Bet Granger; and you're no true lass to give up Will on any terms."

Hester spoke with great vehemence and passion. She was horrified at what she considered sacrilege. She could not understand Bet. Rising from her seat, she pushed her writing materials away, and stooped over the hearth.

"There," she said, as she poked the little fire - "I'm glad as you has spoke out your mind. You hate Dent, and you'll marry him; and you'll give Will his liberty, but you'll break his heart. No, no - I won't write that letter."

"I'll do the best that I can myself," replied Bet. She was not the least angry or excited. She sat down by Hester's table, and taking up the pen dipped it in the ink, and with difficulty began to put her words on paper. Her head was bent low, and her hand labored; but she did not pause, nor glance again at Hester. Minutes passed into half-hours: one - two - three of these went by before Bet, with a burning flush on one cheek, and the other deadly white, finished her letter.

"There," she said. "You don't understand me, Hetty, but I ha' made it all clear to Will. Here's the letter. Seal it up for nought but him to see. When he's free to-morrow, give it to him, Hetty, and don't think harder than you can help of poor Bet Granger."

She laid the letter on the mantel-piece by Hester's side, wrapped her shawl again about her head, and went out.

CHAPTER XXII.

"You ha' got the promise of the girl?" said Dent.

"Yes, yes - that's sure and certain."

"All right; then I'll go to the police-court. Now look you here, Granger - you don't s'pose as I'm *really* going to give that chap his liberty?"

"You won't wed Bet else," replied Granger.

"So *you* say. Well, set down, man. We has half-an-hour afore us, and I've got to think one or two things out. Are you quite aware, or must I make it plainer to yer, the only way in which I could let Will out?"

"It don't seem over clear, for sartin," replied Granger. "But you're a clever chap, Dent, and I trusts yer. You'll let the lad out, and you'll wed my gel, and you'll give me my share of the siller. Come, now - that's plain enough, ain't it?"

"*This* is plain," said Dent, knocking the ashes out of his pipe-the two men were loafing together near one of the quays - "this is plain, and this only - that when Will comes out of prison I goes in. I can't prove Will Scarlett innocent without proving myself t'other thing. Is it likely now - you tell me as it's likely - ef I'll lend myself to that sort of plan?"

"Only you said it," replied Granger. "And for sartin my gel won't wed you else."

"And," continued Dent, "when I'm locked up, it won't look too nice for you. There are a few things as 'ull come out about that money as I stole. Ef I'm took up, Liverpool 'ull be a sight too hot for you, Granger. You take my word on that point."

Granger's bloated and red face turned pale. He did not speak at all for a moment. Then he said, slowly: "You has a plan in your head, Isaac Dent; and the sooner you outs with it the better it'll be for you and for me."

"Yes," said Dent, smiling. "You're about right there, mate. I has a plan, and this is it - I mean to go to the police-court to-day - I means to witness there; but not for Will Scarlett, but *agin'* him. He'll swear as I give him the notes; I'll swear tother way. His case looks black now - I'll make it of a double-dyed darkness. I'll do for him. That'll be none so difficult."

"But what about Bet?" said Granger. "I don't care about Scarlett. It's nought to me how long he stays in prison. But how'll you get Bet to wed you, ef you treats the lad so, is more nor I can make out."

"We'll blind her," said Dent. "Throw dust in her eyes - eh? That's where you can help me, Granger - and five pound, not in notes, but gold, for the job."

Granger looked dubious.

"Bet's going to the police-court," he said.

"She mustn't go - no, not on no account. Look here, Granger, you wern't, so to say, special tender and fatherly to them boys o' yourn, were you?"

"What now?" said Granger.

"Well, just this," replied Dent. "I want you to take them boys, and manage so as Bet shall have a hint of it, and pretend as you're going to do bad by them. Take them out of her sight. She'll follow - she'll spend all the time, while Will's little business is being settled, looking for the boys. It can be done, and we'll lure her out of Liverpool, and we'll pretend as Will is free, until such time as I can wed her. Then I don't care what she knows. Come into the 'Star and Garter,' mate - we'll have a drink, and soon fix up this yer business."

CHAPTER XXIII.

It sometimes happens that a very valiant and resolute spirit is contained in a small body. Bet Granger's little brothers, known in the slums as the captain and the general, were as thin, as lanky, as under-grown little chaps as could be found in Liverpool. Not a scrap of superfluous flesh had they, and certainly not an iota of superfluous growth. They were under-fed, under-sized; but nevertheless brave spirits shone out of their eyes, and valiant and even martial ideas animated their small frames. The "Cap'n" and the "Gen'ral" were considered so plucky by the other boys - and girls of the neighborhood that as a rule they were asked to take the command in a fight, and to assume leading and distinguished positions in a general fray. Most valiantly then would they strike out left or right - regardless of black eyes, indifferent to bumps or blows. They looked like little furies on these occasions, and the other children applauded and admired. It was well known in Sparrow Street, and it was even beginning to be recognized as a certain fact in Paradise Row, that when both the captain and the general were engaged together in one encounter there was not the smallest chance of the opposite side winning.

These untrained and somewhat desperate little bravos had also certain instincts which taught them to espouse the cause of those weaker than themselves: and it was

L. T. Meade

often a ludicrous as well as a pathetic sight to see these small champions leading the van, and eagerly supporting girls and boys a great deal bigger than themselves. Their mother had certainly told them that fighting was sinful; but it was the breath of life to them, and when Thady was once asked what he liked best in the world, he answered promptly, "Punchin' another feller's head." These small boys were quite little braves in their way; but, as there is a weak point in the most invincible armor, so were there conditions under which the general and his gallant captain would undoubtedly show the white feather. There was a presence which could effectually quench the ardor of two pairs of keen eyes, could cause two little faces to blanch to an unwholesome and sickly hue, could cause two little hearts to beat anxiously, and could so affect the moral equilibrium of two very steadfast little souls, that lies would fall glibly from their lips, and the coward's weapons of deceit and subterfuge would be gladly used by them in self-defence.

It was a father who had this effect upon his children; and the torturing and ruining of these young child-lives was being effected in the civilized England of our nineteeth century. Granger represented a not too uncommon type of man, and Nat and Thady did not suffer more than hundreds of other boys when exposed to his influence.

On the morning after Bet had written her letter to Will, she rose early, and was preparing to go to the police-court, to look her last on her lover, when the door of their one little room in Sparrow Street was burst rudely open, and Granger, his face red and bloated, and his whole manner indicating that he had reached the quarrelsome stage of insobriety, entered the room with heavy strides. He was a big man, powerfully made, and when in his present condition even Bet thought it wisest to let him alone. He entered the room and glared about him savagely. A great deal of this manner was put on, for he was acting a part under Dent's instructions; but none of his children knew this, and when striding across the room, he caught the poor little blue-eyed captain by his ragged collar, the boy uttered a scream, and the general, basely deserting his brother, rushed to Bet for protection.

"Give up that lad," shouted Granger, hoarsely. "I want the two of 'em. They are my lads, and you have played the fool with 'em long enough. I have got work as 'ull suit them, away in Warrington, and I'm going to take 'em by an early train. There - hands off, Bet - give me the lads." "Never," cried Bet. She looked like a wild creature about to be deprived of her young. Holding one arm firmly round the general, she gripped the little captain by the other hand.

"Gi' them up to me, father! You shan't have them - you shan't touch them - there! What do you mean? You take 'em away to work at I knows not what? - and they no more nor seven years old! Let 'em be - they're my lads, and you shan't harm a hair of their heads."

The boys clung to her, with white faces. The man, savage and amazed at this unexpected resistance, stood wavering for an instant. At that moment it seemed to Bet as if a thousand furies possessed her, and a thousand strengths were given to her. All the accumulated anguish of the past week seemed to gather vehemence now, and to lend iron force to her muscular arms. She wrenched the little captain quite away from the red-faced, bloated man; and then, both arms freed

L. T. Meade

for a moment, she actually pushed him before her to the door, and, before he could utter a word, or collect his scattered forces, she locked him out.

"There! lads," she said, turning round with a triumphant half laugh, "you see as Bet's as good as her word."

"You're a born fighter," said the captain, in a tone of admiration. He recovered his spirits and his courage on the spot, and in a few moments he and the general were amusing themselves in acting the scene which Bet had just gone through.

"Boys," said their sister's voice, after ten minutes had passed, and no attack been made on the door, she concluded that Granger had for the present withdrawn himself - "Boys, I'm a wanting to go out."

"Oh, no, Bet, no - father'll come back."

"But the door's werry strong. I'll lock it from the outside, and make off with the key. I won't be long, boys; I'm a hungered to see somebody - my heart draws me, and I'm in pain. You won't be in any danger, dear lads, and I'll be back werry soon. I jest want to set eyes on one face that I'll never see no more. You won't be afeard, ef there's a locked door between you and father."

The rare tears which scarcely ever came to her stood in Bet's eyes.

"No, we won't be afeard," said the captain, running up to his sister - "there ain't nought to be afeard of. You're wanting to see your sweetheart - ain't yer, Bet?"

"No," said Bet, with an almost-cry - "I han't got a sweetheart now. All the same, I hungers for the sight of a face. And I'll be back soon. Don't you be fretting, lads. There'll be a locked door atween you and harm."

She wrapped her shawl about her, waited for no further words, locked the door on the little prisoners, and rushed downstairs. As she said, her heart was drawing her. Nothing but that passionate hunger would have caused her to forsake the children at this supreme moment. The house was intensely quiet, for most of the lodgers had gone out on their day's avocations. Not a sign of Granger was to be seen.

Bet walked fast, and presently reached the police-court, where Will was to be tried. A crowd of people were waiting outside; a few policemen stood about. The doors of the building were not yet open. Bet saw Hester Wright standing very near the entrance. She made an effort to get to her, and called her name over the heads of the crowd; but Hester, after looking at her coldly, turned her back without making any response. This action cut Bet to the quick. She found the tears again springing to her eyes. Oh! for one glance, if only the last, of Will's kind face. The minutes dragged themselves along; the crowd increased; but as the right hour had not yet come, the doors remained fast shut. At last, at the stroke of ten, they were opened, and Bet was pressing in with the rest, when she felt a hand laid heavily on her arm. She turned, to see the coarse black-eyed girl who had bought her beat from Granger.

"Ef I was you, I'd go home, Bet," said the girl.

"You mind your own business," said Bet, shaking her off roughly.

"Well - there's a mischief brewing, and I saw what I saw. Don't you say as you wasn't warned; and ef the two little chaps come to grief, it ain't Louisa Perkins' fault."

These last words alarmed Bet.

"Say out yer say at once," she answered, clutching the girl now, and forcing her back against the crowd who were pushing their way into the building, - "say your say and have done," she repeated. "What has come to the lads? I left them safe not an hour agone."

"I saw Granger making off with them."

"You didn't - that's a lie! I left them locked up safe in my room."

"Granger was hurrying off with them," repeated Louisa, "werry red in the face, and mad like. The captain was crying, and t'other chap had a red mark down his cheek - it's not a quarter of an hour by St. Giles' clock as I saw him."

"Where was they going?" asked Bet. "Tell me quick, or I'll shake you."

"Down Castle Street, making for Lime Street and the railway station, I expect."

Bet ceased to push inwards with the crowd. They went past her, and the little police-court was soon filled to overflowing. Isaac Dent almost rubbed against her shoulder as he went by. He winked at Louisa, but Bet never noticed him.

"Hester - Hester Wright!" she suddenly called out.

Hester had not yet gone into the police-court. She was standing against one of the posts of the door, watching the crowd as they filed past.

"Hester!" repeated Bet. "Hetty - Hetty! Come and speak to me for a minute! I must go, but I want to send a message. Just one word, Hetty, - Hetty, come!"

Perhaps Hester did not hear. At any rate, she neither turned nor heeded. Bet gave a low despairing cry; then, flinging her shawl off her shoulders, she ran as fast as if there were wings to her feet in the direction of Sparrow Street.

L. T. Meade

CHAPTER XXIV.

She reached her destination very quickly. The smooth-faced landlord was standing at the door.

"Eh! is that you, Bet Granger?" he exclaimed. "Eh - you are in a taking. You might stop a minute to pass a civil good-morning with a chap. Well, what a gel that is! But ain't she handsome - just."

Bet flew past him like a whirlwind, and his last words were addressed to the empty air. Three pairs up she ran, her breath coming quicker and quicker. On the landing she paused, and pressed her hand to her wildly beating heart. It was all quite true. Louisa Perkins had not told her a lie. The room door stood wide open; the room itself was empty.

"Boys!" she called, when she could gather breath to speak. "Little lads, I ha' come back to you! You needn't hide no more, for Bet's yere."

But she knew as she said the words that the boys were not hiding. They had fallen into the clutches of the oppressor - they had gone. She went slowly now into the deserted room. She was waiting for her breath to return, for her heart to beat easily, to commence her search. Yes: that was the only duty left to her in life - to find the boys and redeem her promise to her mother.

She sat down on a chair, and wiped her heated forehead, and gradually made her plans. First of all she would go to Mother Bunch - and then, then - away to Warrington. Warrington was not a big place; it would be impossible for Granger to elude her long there. Could she once again find the lads she need not greatly fear her father. After all she had nearly, if not quite, his physical strength; and she believed that if it came to a personal encounter between them, her muscles, joined to her woman's wit, would give her the victory.

Opening the front of her dress, she pulled out a hand-kerchief, and, unknotting it, looked at the little money in her possession. The handkerchief only contained a few pence - certainly not the price of a third-class fare to Warrington. As she was leaving the room, however, she caught a hidden gleam on the little deal dresser. She ran to it and picked up half-a-crown. How had it got there? She had no time to think of that; it was hers now, to use as she thought best. She would go to Mother Bunch first. That worthy was offended with her; but what of that, she must soothe Mother Bunch's temper, make her once more her friend, get her to look out for any tidings of the boys, and then go on her wildgoose chase to Warrington.

Whenever Mother Bunch was not eating, sleeping, or scolding some one, she was engaged over the wash-tub. It might have puzzled an outsider to know what results she achieved from such arduous labor, for she scorned to take in washing as a profession; and neither she nor her good man, a certain lanky-looking Patrick O'Flaherty, were remarkable for the whiteness of their linen, or the general cleanliness of their apparel.

Mother Bunch washed and washed, hanging out

numerous garments to dry, rinsing the suds from her own arms, rendering her small kitchen damp and messy at all hours, and during all seasons. She scarcely raised her head when Bet entered. The soft sound of the soapy water and the gentle splash of the dripping garments greeted the girl as an accustomed sound, and Mother Bunch's broad back was reassuring.

"Oh, Mrs. O'Flaherty," said Bet, running up to her, putting her arms round her neck, and imprinting a kiss on her soapy forehead. "I'm in a sight of trouble, and I've come to you to help me."

"Glory! child, don't stand right in the way of the soap suds! There you go - splashing all the clothes, and I'll have to wash 'em all over again. Oh, dearie, dearie me - my heart's broke, and that's the truth I'm telling ye. Well, honey - and so ye comes back to Mother Bunch when you want a rale drop of consolation. You know as the old Irishwoman's your frind, and don't bear no malice."

"I know that, Mother Bunch! I think now I did wrong to take the lads away from you - only I did it for the best."

"Well, now, honey, I wouldn't say that ef I was you. You did it for love, and love's contrairey. But don't talk to me of doing it for the best. How's that broth of a boy, Scarlett? Have you got your own way about him, lovey?"

"Yes," said Bet. "Will has got his liberty by now." Her face turned white. "We won't talk of that; there was a price to be paid and it's paid. Will is free, that's a comfort."

"Yes," said Mother Bunch. "But there's a sore thrubble on ye, honey. I see it in your eyes. I'm glad the lad's free. Ef they consailed a lad like that in prison - why it would have been the death of him, my dear. Will's the boy that must have his liberty. I expect you'll find him quare and altered, even after one week of prison, Bet."

Bet's face brightened, "I'm glad that you, too, understand Will," she said. "I knew that the prison would kill my lad. He's free now."

"And why arn't you with him, honey? Why, it's an iligant wedding you ought to be having together, and Mother Bunch dancing an Irish jig, and pouring down blessings on the heads of two of yez. Come now, Bet, what's up? Spake your mind free to the old Irishwoman."

"I have nothing to tell, and I can't wait," said Bet. "Father have took away the two lads, and I'm follering of him. He said he would take them to Warrington. I'm a-going arter him, and I'll fetch them back; only I thought I'd tell you, Mother Bunch, so as you might keep your ears open, and let me know ef there's any tidings or news going. Father may have said Warrington jest to deceive me, for he's awful deep, and the lads may be here all the time. You keep your eyes open, and your ears too, Mother Bunch, and I'll come back to you in a day or so ef I can't find them. Now, good-bye - I'm off, I want to catch a train."

Bet found herself at Warrington soon after one o'clock.

She was landed on the platform and stood looking round her in a bewildered way. The place was totally strange, and she felt like a deserted vessel cast adrift

L. T. Meade

from its usual moorings. There was no part of Liverpool where she would not know what to do and how to act; but here, standing on this lonely, deserted platform, with scarcely any money in her pocket, her head aching, her tired brain dull and confused, she scarcely knew where to turn. If her father were really here with the children, it might not be such a very easy task to find them.

She was startled by a familiar, half-mocking, half-exultant voice at her elbow. She turned quickly, and there stood the sailor, Isaac Dent.

"Ha, ha! sweetheart!" he said. "I wasn't long in a-follering of you up - was I? And you're mine now, my beautiful Bet. You're mine, and no mistake."

Bet's eyes flashed, and her face grew crimson, - it was as much as she could do to restrain the impulse to raise her hand, and strike Dent. But then she recollected herself. After all, she did belong to this man, and Will's liberty was the price. "You know my terms," she said, when she could find her voice to speak. "Is my lad free? Ef my lad's not free as the air - I'll - ! Tell me that afore I have any more words with you."

Dent laughed; he was in exuberant spirits.

"Your lad!" he repeated. "It seems to me as I'm your lad. Name the feller you mean in some other way afore I answers any saucy questions. You're a fine young woman, Bet, but you has to go Isaac Dent's way now. What's the name of the feller you wants me to tell you about?"

"Will Scarlett - is he out of prison?" replied the girl.

She swallowed a deep breath, and her face was white and cold as marble.

"Yes; Will Scarlett's free," answered Dent "He's out of prison, in course, and he's free as the air. All owing to that good feller Dent standing up for him, and witnessing for him, and proving him as innercent as the babe unborn. My word! - worn't he glad to get his liberty. And didn't he wring my hand, and say, 'God bless you, my boy!' You sent him a letter, Bet, and he read it, and gived me a line or two to take to you. You'd know Will's fist ef you see'd it on an envelope now - wouldn't you?"

"I can't say," replied Bet. "Give me his letter!"

"All in good time, my pretty - all in werry good time! Shall we walk down the street a bit? You're obliged to poor Isaac Dent, now, ain't you, Bet? He have done his part by Will Scarlett, haven't he?"

"Yes, Isaac. I'm much obleeged to yer. I'm glad as Will is free. Give me the letter what he writ to me, please."

"I will, by-and-bye. You have got to forget him now. You're mine now - you remember as that's the bargain?"

"Yes, Isaac, I remember - I'll wed you as soon as you can fix up the license. Oh, I'm glad that Will is free! Did he look awful bad and changed, Isaac?"

"Bad?" repeated Dent. "Yaller as a guinea, - awful, he look - but he'll be better soon. He said to me, 'Another week o' this, and I'd ha' been a dead man, Dent - bless you, Dent, old pal' said Will - 'and take the gel and my blessing too. She was right, Bet wor - liberty's more nor anything else to a sailor chap. Oh, yes - I'll miss her; for she was rare and handsome; but, lord there's plenty of other good fish in the sea;' and then he writ this letter, and give it me - jest a line or two, to make it all square atween you and me, as he said. And he'll come and see us arter his next voyage, he said. Here's the letter, Bet - and obleeged you ought to be to me, sweetheart."

"Thank you, Isaac," replied Bet.

She took Will's letter with a hand that trembled, and thrust it unopened into the bosom of her dress.

"It wor what I wanted," she muttered, half under her breath. "All the same I'm stunned like. Isaac, I ha' come here to find father and the lads. Father has made off with the two boys, and he dropped a hint about bringing 'em here."

"Werry like he did," replied Dent. "He dropped a hint to me about making a tidy penny or so out of them boys round yere. Ef you stay for a day or two, Bet, you'll most likely find them. I'll help you all I can. And Warrington ain't a bad place to stop in. We might be married here - why not? I know a decent gel here what'll share her room with you - we'll go and find her now."

CHAPTER XXV.

Dent soon made terms with the girl who was to accommodate Bet with half her room. Her terms were half-a-crown a week, which Dent offered to provide. Bet, however, scowled at him.

"None o' that" she said. "I ain't your wife yet - and I can't be, neither, thank goodness, for a fortnight. Jenny here says I may go round with her and help her to hawk her basket. I'll help Jenny with her bits of cress and vegetables-and I want no help from you."

"You're a proud 'un," said Dent, "but I'll break yer in yet."

He spoke more angrily than he had meant. Bets cheeks grew white; he was turning away, but she followed him.

"Listen, Isaac," she said. "I'm not your wife yet; and by the laws of England I can't be for a fortnight. It was them laws as parted me and Will - cruel, I thought them - bitter cruel. Him and me would have been mated together, and safe and happy - oh, yes! we two would have been happy but for them laws which we mustn't break, if we was to be honest and true man and woman. And them same laws stand good still, Isaac Dent; and I can't come to you to be wedded to you under a fortnight. They was cruel once - now they're kind; they gives me a fortnight afore I steps into a state what will be worse nor death to me - ay, worse than the cold grave! We must wait a fortnight, Dent - you must wait a whole fourteen days afore you take to bullying me. And, listen, Dent - I'm a despert girl. I have lost all that makes life worth anything. You trust me 'cause you know it's said everywhere as Bet Granger keeps true to her word through all things. But I ha' broke a promise already made most solemn to my mother when she lay a-dying; and ef you tries me too far, and don't do what I wish for the next fortnight afore we can come together - why, I'll fling my word back in your face, and dare you to do your worst. I'm despert - evn my word ain't much to me, now. And I'll do it, Isaac, I'll do it; I'll declare as I'll never, never be wed to you! You can't harm me - you can't force me. And Will's free now. You could never touch me at all except through Will. And now my lad's free, and the salt sea will soon blow the prison look out of his face. You haven't got me yet, Isaac Dent: so you had better humor me for the next fortnight."

Dent's unwholesome face became much mottled and disturbed in hue during Bet's speech. When she spoke of Will being free, his lips took an ugly sneer, and he found extreme difficulty in restraining himself. He was well aware, however, that if he disclosed the fact of his own treachery his last hope of winning this proud lass was over. After all, nothing held her to him but her promise; and if she came to regard promises in the same light in which he did, all his pains and troubles would be thrown away. If he wished to win her, it behoved him, therefore, to be cautious, and, as she put it very plainly, to humor her. After the wedding day all the self-restraint which he must at present exhibit might be withdrawn. His feelings for Bet contained a curious mixture of anger and fierce admiration. It never occurred to him for a moment even to try to make her a good husband; but get her he would - oh, yes - possess her he must.

When she harangued him thus, with her eyes flashing, and a world of scorn curving her beautiful lips, he replied gently, drawing close to her, but not offering to touch her.

"I'll do anything in my power to please you, Bet," he said. "I ain't a bad sort - my bark's worse nor my bite. I'm not a polished diamond. But ef I don't make you a good husband, and ef you and me won't have the jolliest little house in Liverpool together, my name ain't Dent - no - my name ain't Dent. You trust me, Bet - I'll not anger you either now nor in the future. What is it you wants me to do?"

"To leave me alone," said Bet, "until you can fetch the license and bring me to church with you. Ef I was to see too much of you atween now and our wedding, no promise that ever was would bind me. You keep away, Isaac, and leave me my fortnight in peace, and I'll do what I said I'd do - yes, I'll do it - I'll pay the price. You go back to Liverpool, Isaac, and leave me yere - I has to find father and the lads. And ef Jenny's a good sort, I'll stay with her. Ef she ain't, I'll find my own lodging. But in no case will I walk with you, or talk with you, until the day as we is wed. Ef I stays here for a fortnight we can be wed here, but you must go back to Liverpool. Them's my terms, and if you don't humor me for the present, - why, you know what to look for."

"Oh, I'm agreed," answered Dent, "I'll humor you now,

L. T. Meade

and I'll humor you in the future. I suppose we can be married before the register. You don't want no church words over yer, - do you, Bet?"

"No, not when I stand by *your side*," said Bet, shuddering.

"Well, I'll do yer pleasure. I'll go now, and make inquiries, and enter our names to be wed as soon as may be. Liverpool 'ull suit me a deal better than this dull hole of a Warrington. Goodbye, my fine lady Bet - when next we meets, it 'ull be never to part."

He kissed the tips of his fingers to her, and could not resist a laugh which sounded between mockery and triumph.

As Dent turned away, Bet's attention was arrested by the girl called Jenny, who had been standing by during this colloquy, and plucked her by the sleeve.

"Yer a rare 'un!" she said, in a tone of sincere admiration. "Don't you mate with him. He ain't fit for the likes of you. Break your word with him, - what's a lie or two?"

"I hate lies," said Bet in a voice of scorn. "Let me be, Jenny - you're right in what you say of Isaac Dent; but he have my promise, and I ain't one as lies, ef it's only myself I have to think on."

"Yer a rare 'un," repeated Jenny. She was small and squat, with a broad, freckled face, and light blue, saucer eyes. She looked up at the handsome girl by her side with the most sincere admiration.

"Lor! you have the courage," she said. "I'll be proud to go a-hawking with you."

Jenny's most commonplace appearance - her homely words - had a soothing effect on Bet.

"I'll go with you presently. Jenny," she answered. "But now may I go to your room, and may I stay alone there - for - for - say an hour?"

Jenny's beaming face fell. In her rough, untutored heart she had already conceived an affection for Bet. She would have dearly liked to sit in her very dirty attic bedroom, and gossip with her. That would have been nearly as good as walking through the streets of Warrington in company with so distinguished a companion. To walk through the streets, the envied of all, with Bet by her side would have been a crowning triumph for the poor little hawker, Jenny; but to give her up her room, - not to see her at all for a whole hour, - was a far less agreeable matter.

"Oh, I'll do it," she said. "You're welcome to the room. It ain't for me to make no objections."

She spoke summarily, and with some bitterness of spirit, but Bet was far too much absorbed in her own meditations to notice her.

When Jenny finally closed the door of her apartment, and unwillingly sauntered downstairs, Bet drew Will's letter from its hiding-place. She tore it open, and her feverish bright eyes devoured the few lines it contained. These were thewords with which Will bade his sweetheart good-bye:

"Dear Bet, - Isaac Dent will take you my farewell. I am free, and I means to find a berth in the first ship as leaves the docks as 'ull take me on board. Dear Bet - I was innercent as the babe unborn - but it was Dent as cleared me. He spoke as a man, dear Bet, and I was proud to think as we was pals once on board The Albion ship when it sailed over the dancing waves. He's not a feller to let a comrade suffer, is Dent. I got your letter. You was right, Bet - I couldn't a-bear prison, - it was killing me by inches. I'm wasted now almost to a shadder. Dent tells me as you'll soon be wed, and that never may I call you wife o' mine. Bless you and him! I hasn't another word to say. - Will Scarlett."

Bet read this letter with some difficulty. She was, as she said, "a poor scholard," and she had to spread out the sheet of thin paper on Jenny's little bed, and laboriously spell through the words before she could arrive at any true glimpse of their meaning. It dawned upon her, after nearly an hour's severe study, - it dawned upon her just as Jenny's impatient tap came to the door, and her still more impatient voice exclaimed -

"Time's hup - I'm going hawking."

Bet felt herself turning cold and hot, as the meaning of Will's words seemed to scathe and burn her brain. Then, quick as a flash of lightning, another thought came to her, and she smiled, and tore the obnoxious and cruel letter into a thousand little bits.

"That wasn't from my Will," she said. "Dent wrote it - not Will. My lad, - why he jest couldn't put words on paper sech as them! This is Dent's villainy; - yes,

Jenny, I'm a-coming," she called out in quite a cheerful tone.

A weight was lifted from her mind when the conviction became assured that this letter was none of Will's. She went downstairs, and Jenny and she, on the best of terms, commenced their life of hawking together.

Will was free, - no doubt on that point arose to shake her confidence, - but Will's whole nature had not changed. He who possessed the tenderest and the truest heart for her in all the world had not lost it during one week in jail. Bet almost sang as she accompanied Jenny through the Warrington streets. Will was free - freed by her act, - freed by her sacrifice; but a fortnight still stood between her and her doom. For a fortnight, therefore, she could be almost happy, and could at least devote her time to searching for her brothers, and trying to rescue them from the tender mercies of their most cruel father.

CHAPTER XXVI.

Two or three days after Will's second examination before the magistrates-an examination which had ended, owing to Dent's testimony against him, in his being remanded for trial at the coming assizes-Hester Wright was standing in her little room, putting on her shawl and bonnet to go out to her usual day's work. Hester was not at all a model worker; nor had she any of the qualities which ensure commercial success. She was clever all round; and whether it was singing her soul away, or toiling by the hour at shop needlework, or hawking fruit and vegetables about the Liverpool streets, she did a little better than anybody else; but as she would never sell her gift of song, and as her nature was in several respects, notwithstanding its real depth and earnestness, volatile, she could never keep very long to the same mode of earning her bread. A month or two of needlework would be followed by a month or two of hawking: she did not earn more than enough to keep soul and body together by either of these trades; but money and creature comforts were alike matters of indifference to her, and as a rule she preferred the roving life of a hawker, as it brought her more into contact with her fellow creatures. Hawking was in the ascendant now, and she was hurrying out to replenish her basket at St. John's Market when a boy unceremoniously opened her door, and, thrusting a crumpled and dirty piece of paper into her hand, stood staring at her while she opened it.

The letter was a scrawl from Will Scarlett.

"Dear Hetty," it ran, "I may see a friend to-day. Come to me at noon, for I am in a sore taking. - Your cousin Will."

"All right, ain't it?" questioned the boy.

"Yes," replied Hester. "It's from Will. How did you come by it, Davy?"

"John Wheeler gave it to me - he's one of the jailers. He said Will was in a sore way about his lass."

A frown gathered on Hester's brow. "I'll go to him," she said. "Thank you, Davy - the letter's all right."

The boy nodded and vanished, and Hester, taking up her basket, went slowly downstairs.

At twelve o'clock that day she stood by Will's side in his dreary little cell. She was allowed to see him for a few minutes without the presence of a third person. Will had lost somewhat of his bronze; his face was thin and pale; and Hester, going up to him, and clasping his hands, was about to burst forth into a distressful wail at his changed appearance, when he stopped her.

"We ha' no time, Hetty. I know just what your heart's full of, but it's all about Bet we must talk. The time's all too short, and I'm bound hand-and-foot here, and can do nought. See, Hetty-I had a letter from my lass."

"I know, Will ; but it ain't worth your while to fret for

L. T. Meade

her. I know she has gived you up for that Dent fellow; and ef she, what thought to call you mate, can wed with one like him-why, let her, I say. I'm sorry as you're pained, Will; but don't let's waste the minutes talking about one like Bet Granger."

"Hush," said Will. "You say false words, Hetty-I'm 'shamed of you."

Will's blue eyes flashed.

He pulled Bet's letter out of the bosom of his prison shirt, and kissed it passionately.

"She gived me up-poor Bet did," he said. "And that's all you thinked on her! She thought to save me, and she took what would be as death to one like her. I'm 'shamed of you, Hetty. I thought-I did think-that when a gel did an out-and-out grand thing you'd be the first to see it."

Hester colored. Her eyes filled with tears.

"It seemed to me," she said, "as no one what loved you could take up with one like Dent. I may be wrong - I was angered at Bet and I spoke angry. Never mind. It's you as she has wronged - ef you can forgive her, I'll bear no malice."

"I ha' nothing to forgive," said Will. "Forgive? It's all t'other way. She said in her letter, - no, I don't want you to read it, as you doubted her, but this is some o' what she said: 'I give you your freedom, Will. I ain't much, only a lass like any other lass; but freedom - that's all in all to one like you. I remember me how you spoke of the salt breeze blowing on your cheek, and you said the fresh air off the Mersey was nought at all to the fresh air off the ocean, when you was miles and miles away to sea. I give it back to you, dear Will. I'll be Dent's wife, for he won't set you free no other way; but there's many another lass, and I pray that you may wed a good wife, and forget poor Bet.' But I'll never forget her," said Will, who had been reading these extracts in a choking voice, "and I say she's the noblest lass in England, what thinks more of her lad than of herself, and I'm proud of her for writing me like this, for she has let me see down into her heart - and it's a good heart, and strong and pure; and though she don't say no words about it she's the best gel in the land, and ef I gave her up arter reading this letter I'd be the meanest cur that ever sailed, and it's Davy Jones' locker as 'ud be the right place for me, and no other. I'm as innercent as a baby, Hester, and that you know, and so does my gel; and you has got now to turn round, and think on her my way, and help me to save her."

Hester went up close to Will and took one of his hard muscular hands in hers.

"I'll go your way, whether I think it or not," she said. "Let thoughts alone, this is a time for deeds. What do you want me to do, Will?"

"To find Bet," said Will. "She mustn't wed that feller. Thank the good God - she can't for a few days; but time passes, and Dent may have her safe in his clutches afore I know. You has got to find her, Hetty, and you has got to say that William Scarlett will never give her up - that I love her tenfold more than ever for what she thought to do for me; but ef she has promised herself ten times over to that scoundrel Dent, she must tear up them promises, and think nought of them, - for she was mine first, and I refuse to part her. Tell her from me, Hetty, that ef they're the last words I'm ever to speak, much as I love her now, I could curse her - ay, and I would curse her - ef she was to become wife to Dent."

"But she can't, Will," said Hester; "the condition was ef you was set free. Dent did not set you free. He locked you up firmer nor ever in jail, so it ain't likely as Bet, seeing as she loved you, 'ud give herself to him when he only deceived her, and done you an injury?"

"But, a while back," said Will, with a sad smile, "you misdoubted Bet's love for me. I never misdoubted it, nor ever will; but I do misdoubt Dent. He's a coward and a sneak, and deep is no word for him. Ef he wants Bet - and I know he wants her, for he let out as much to me - he'll move heaven and earth to win her, and he'd think nought of deceiving her, and telling her dozens of lies. What does a girl like Bet Granger know of the ways of the world? She has been up and down in the slums, you say, all her life; but there's some as evil can't touch, and she's one of them. Dent, he's full of wickedness, and he knows wicked ways here and wicked ways in other places - so how could a gel like Bet be a match for him? She's brave as a lion. But I can't sleep o' nights thinking how he'll deceive her. He'll let her think as I'm free, and she'll believe him, and he'll cast up her promise to her - and she's terrible over promises, is Bet. You must find her, Hetty, and you mustn't lose an hour, for it's near a week now since the day I was examined last. You must find her and take her my message. Say it any way you like, only let her feel that I'll never, never give her up."

"I'll find her," said Hester. "I'll find her, and speak your words to her. Don't you fret, Will. I ain't your cousin

Hetty, and the most popular singer in the Liverpool slums, for nought. I own I was a bit rough on Bet, and she's a proud lass, and wouldn't come nigh me ef she thought I was angered, or took her the wrong way. Maybe I judged her wrong - maybe I didn't - we won't go into that. When I meets her now I'll promise to be gentle, and I'll keep her for you, cousin, ef such a thing's possible, and I'll save her from that scoundrel, ef such a thing's possible. You trust her to me. But now, one word about yourself, Will. You has been done a bitter wrong, and you don't look spry - no, you don't look spry."

"It was Dent," said Will. "I see it all now. It was a scheme of his to win my gel from me. I don't suppose as I'll be acquitted, Hetty, and they say as I'll have two year. Well, I ain't the first innercent man as has been done by a rogue; no, nor the last neither. You tell Bet to keep up heart, for, even if it is two year, I'll come to her at the end, and we'll be none the worse, seeing that we know each other and love each other as we do. Good-bye, Hetty - I hear the warder coming. That bit of a verse you sang keeps running in my head, and it soothes me wonderful when I get most mad, like. You remember it - 'Oh, rest in the Lord, wait patiently for Him!'"

"And He will give thee thy heart's desire," said Hester. Her eyes lit up, and she half sang, half chanted the words.

"Seems as if He might." she said. "Not as I holds with no goodness; but them words, they fasten on to me, and I can't rid myself neither of them or of their meaning. Good-bye, Will. I'll do my best, not only for Bet, but to set you free again."

CHAPTER XXVII.

When Hester left the jail she went straight to Sparrow Street. She knew that Bet had gone back there, and felt pretty certain either that she would see the girl herself or be able to leave a message for her with one of the other lodgers. She climbed the three pair of stairs, and knocked at the door of Bet's room. A voice, not Bet's, invited her in, and she found herself in a cloud of tobacco-smoke, and in the presence of both Granger and Dent, who were lounging one on each side of the fire, smoking very coarse tobacco, and imbibing beer from a great jug which stood on a little deal table between them.

Both men started, and removed their pipes from their mouth, when Hester entered.

"Well, Hetty, what's your pleasure?" asked Granger, in a would-be facetious tone. "Going, Dent?" For the younger man had risen to his feet and was preparing to leave the room.

"Yes, I may as well see to that matter by the docks," mumbled Dent, as he made for the door. Hester stepped between it and him.

"A word with you first, Isaac," she said, in that rich, peculiar voice of hers. " I want to speak with

Bet - where is she?"

Hester laid her hand on the man's shoulder.

"Where's the girl, Elizabeth Granger, Isaac Bent?" she said. "Tell me that much, and then you can go."

Dent laughed disagreeably.

"Hands off, Hetty," he said. "Bless yer! What do *I* know of Elizabeth Granger? Ask her father - he's there - the girl ain't nought to me. Stand away from the door, Hetty Wright - I'm in no end of a hurry."

"So am I, and so is Will," said Hetty, without budging an inch." We want Bet - we want the gel what you, Isaac Dent, has stolen away. She was Will's - she was his promised wife, and the good words 'most read over them, and they was very nearly wed. You stepped atween them, and stole her from Will. You're a thief out and out, - you take away a man's character from him, and you part him from his lass as well as stealing bank-notes and sealskin purses from ladies. Oh - I know you! And I'd rather be Will, lying in prison this minute, than I'd be you. Yes, you can go now, for I ha' said my say, and I'd never get the truth out of you ef I was to wait here forever But I'll find Bet, and she shan't be your wife if I can help it. I ain't a singer for nothing; I ain't the most popular singer in the slums for nought. So you needn't defy me; for if I like I can make matters hot for you."

Hester had not only now moved away from the door, but she had flung it open, and Dent, muttering much, with his face white, and a very hangdog expression on it, slunk down the stairs. He said to himself: "There ain't no use in life bandying words with her; and it's true what she says - there ain't a man or woman in Liverpool what wouldn't do her bidding."

When Dent was gone Hester went up to Granger, and, altering her tactics, began to ask him what he knew about Bet. The man was looking up at her in dull surprise, and with an expression of heavy, open-mouthed admiration.

"You did tackle him, Het," he said. "My word! - you has a way with you, lass."

"Let me use it on you, then, Mr. Granger," said Hetty. "I want Bet - where be she?"

"What will you give me ef I tell you?"

"I haven't much to give. I can sing to yer - tell me, and I'll give you the bonniest song - one that no bird in springtime could beat."

"Ay, ay, lass," said Granger. "You know your power, and how you can wheedle anything out of a fellow; but the fact is I don't know where Bet is hiding; and if I did the secret is Dent's, not mine. But I don't - so there. What's the matter, Hester? - what are you staring at? - oh, that child - you let him alone, he's asleep, that child is. I popped him into bed, and he's asleep. You let him be, Hester Wright."

"I will, when I've looked at him," said Hester.

She moved over to the bed, on which a forlorn little figure lay prone. A white cheek pressed the pillow, and two big blue eyes looked up imploringly at Hester.

"Why, it's the cap'n!" said the singer, bending over the boy, and pushing the bright reddish hair off his forehead. "What are you doing, laddie? - and where's your brother?"

The captain's eyes said unutterable things, but his lips did not move - Granger as well as Hester was watching his face.

"He's resting - can't yer see it?" said the man. "You let him go back to his sleep. His brother? - oh, he's out larking in the street."

A curious look came over Hester's face. Her manner completely altered. Stooping again, she pressed a very light kiss on the boy's white cold brow.

"Go to sleep, lad," she said.

Then she turned to Granger.

"I won't trouble you to tell me about Bet," she said, in her most conciliatory tones. "Ef it's Dent's secret, I know as you ain't to blame. There's many a hard thing said about a person what hasn't a word of truth in it. I believe you're a right good man, Mr. Granger. Well, I must go off, for I'd like to get news of Bet, but ef you like I'll come back to-night and sing to you."

"Will you?" said Granger, eagerly. "There's nothing like a song, and somehow, your voice goes through a feller. I'll collect a few neighbors, and we'll have a bit of supper and a fine time. What hour'll you come, Hetty?"

"When the clock's gone seven," said Hester.

L. T. Meade

"I mightn't be in then, - I sometimes gets an odd job, and I may to-night, down by the docks; but I'll leave the room-door on the latch, and you can come in when you please. The boy? Oh, he's well enough. You won't mind hearing Hetty sing, will you, cap'n?"

Again the blue eyes looked up piteously, but the little white lips were silent. Hester nodded, and smiled brightly at Granger.

"I'll look in as soon as I can," she repeated. "You leave the door on the latch."

Then she tripped downstairs; she had not even glanced again in the direction of the little captain.

"Now to see Mother Bunch," said Hester to herself. "There's no doubt as my hands 'ull be full for the next few days; but I think I see a way of getting the better of Dent, and of Granger too, - see ef I don't - oh! that poor child - that poor, poor child!"

At the corner of the street, leaning half tipsily against the wall, stood the old hag to whom Hester had once given twopence. Her eyes brightened when she saw who was walking down the street.

"God bless yer, Hetty Wright!" she mumbled.

Hester was accustomed to many such exclamations; they always had a power over her, and brought a light into her eyes. She stopped now in front of the old woman.

"Thank you, Mrs. Flannigan. These are hard times with you, I fear."

"So they be, dearie - so they be. I haven't taken sixpence this blessed day, and 'tis bitter cold standing about, and with not much chance of a shelter before yon for the night."

"I have thought of something," said Hester. "I'll be very busy for the next few days, and I'd like to have my hands free. Will you carry round my basket for me, mother? I'll go to the market and get it filled for you every morning, and you'll give me the change at night. You shall have a third of what you earns. One-third goes for stock - one to me, one to you. It's better nor nought; and ef you say an' it's Hester Wright's basket, folks 'ull buy, for they know as my cresses and oranges ain't to be beat in Liverpool."

The old woman's eyes absolutely danced as Hester made her this offer.

"And I won't cheat you of a farthing, darling," she exclaimed. "Oh, but it's you as is the blessing of God to me!"

"Come home with me, then," said Hester. "The basket is in my room, and the things unsold, - come at once, for I'm in a rare bit of a hurry."

Having disposed of old Mrs. Flannigan, and in this manner secured for herself as well as for the dame a means of livelihood for the next few days, Hester started off for Paradise Row. It was a fact that there was not a more dishonest nor evil-minded old woman in Liverpool than this same Mrs. Flannigan; but Hester was firmly convinced that she would be true to her word, and not rob her of a farthing, and this proved to be the case.

As usual Mother Bunch was bending over her wash-tub. Her broad back was turned to Hester as she entered the little room. Even in Paradise Row the singer was not quite unknown, and Mother Bunch gave her a welcoming word. Hester soon poured out her story, which was received with many exclamations, and such growing and deepening interest that the wash-tub was forgotten and the Irishwoman stood with her arms a-kimbo, fairly panting with indignation and excitement.

"Oh, the villains! - oh, the black-hearted creatures!" she exclaimed once or twice. "Right you are, Hetty, - you have got Mother Bunch on your side, and I have got an ahrum - see, honey, - I'll do whatever you bids me, darlint, - but I'll save Bet and the poor children."

"Listen, then, Mother Bunch," said Hester. "You tell me that Bet has left Liverpool. Can you not try and remember where she said she was going?"

"She didn't tell me, dear. She didn't let out nought. Only it worn't far away. Too far to walk, honey, and the train was to take the poor child. Some miles off - maybe fifteen - maybe a score; but railly I can't remember. I ain't good at mintal 'rithmetic, darlint."

"Never mind about that now," said Hester; "we have to think of the cap'n first, and of how to outwit Dent. Now, listen. I have got an idea in the back of my head."

Here Hester began to talk in a very low voice, and Mother Bunch listened, nodding vehement approval, chuckling audibly once or twice, grinning broadly at other times, and throwing out several practical and shrewd suggestions of her own. Before Hester left Paradise Row the two had come to a complete understanding.

"I'll have his poor sisther's room as snug as snug for him," said Mother Bunch, in conclusion. "Oh, he'll be safe there. You trust me that-he'll be safe there!"

"And I'll sit up with him to-night," said Hester. "Well - all right, Mrs. O'Flaherty, I'll meet you at a quarter to seven at the corner of Sparrow Street."

There are times when it is dreadful to be quite alone - when the head reels, and the floor seems to sink down beneath one, and the solid earth seems no longer firm and supporting. And when one is very young, and, although the battle of life has gone hard, the years that have passed over our heads are only a few, and we feel that we ought to be petted and loved, and made much of, and held tenderly in our mother's arms, with that tired, weary, drooping little head resting on her breast, - then the loneliness is very hard to bear, and the brave child-heart cries in terror, and wonders if God no longer suffers little children to come to Him.

The captain was very weak and ill. He had gone through a cruel time, - he did not want to think of it, - he was lying all alone in bed, quite alone, with a few flickering shadows from the dying fire reflecting a light on the walls, and making grim shadows, too, which frightened him so much that he liked best to lie with his eyes shut.

His father would come back presently, - it was far worse to have his father there than to lie alone in the dark - only, why did his head feel so queer, and why

L. T. Meade

were his hands so feeble? He did not think he could punch anyone now; and as to being victor in a fight, why - even Dan Davis, the weakest boy of his acquaintance, and one for whom he had the greatest contempt, would have been a match for him.

Still, it was very dull being alone, and the room seemed to grow darker, and his head lighter. He was thirsty, but there was nothing to drink. Where was Bet? Where was the general? He opened his little lips to call these friendly and protecting names, but no audible sound would come from them.

Oh, what was the matter? He was really frightened now - even his father's presence would have been better than nothing. Who and what was that? There was a noise on the stairs - the room door opened, and the large face and solid tub-like form of Mother Bunch seemed suddenly to fill the whole apartment. The poor little captain found sudden vent for one weak cry of rapture, then he fainted away.

CHAPTER XXVIII.

The captain was very ill, but he was no longer uncared for. In the attic which Bet had rendered clean and sweet, he lay and tossed on his hard and feverish bed. His weakness and prostration were difficult to account for; he could give no coherent account of himself, only, as the fever left him false strength, he murmured his brother's name continually, telling him to hide, to run fast, and promising to overtake him as soon as possible. Once or twice he screamed piteously, as though he were again feeling the hard strokes of a cruel hand. The doctor came to see him, and ordered lots of nourishment, and spoke gravely of the boy's state.

"Why is not his sister with him?" the medical man said; for he knew Bet, and had often remarked her kindness and tenderness to her young brothers.

In the absence of Bet, however, the captain was not neglected, Mother Bunch taking care of him by day, and at all times when Hester Wright was obliged to be absent. There were no traces anywhere of the poor little general. It is true he might still be at Sparrow Street, but Hester thought it wiser for many reasons not to venture there just now.

If Granger was in a taking about the kidnapping of his

L. T. Meade

little son, he certainly showed no symptoms of invading Mother Bunch's premises on his behalf; and it was thought best for the captain's sake to do nothing to rouse his father's ire at present.

"We'll have him by-and-bye - he shall feel this ahrum yet," said Mother Bunch. "But now you and me has got to pull this child through, Hetty Wright. It do seem to me that he's 'most took for death, but we'll pull him through by the help of God Almighty."

This was no easy matter; for the little life seemed to be ebbing further and further away from this world's shores, and often it seemed to Hester that the unconscious child scarcely breathed.

"I wouldn't like Bet to come back, and not see the little chap," she replied once to Mother Bunch, who was gazing at him with a very dubious look on her face. "Ef there ever was a good sister, Bet's the one; and I wouldn't like her to come here and see no captain - and, for that matter, no general neither."

"We'll pull him through," said Mother Bunch. "Even if he is took for death - we'll pull him through."

She always said this, although her tones of late had grown less confident.

On this occasion she took Hester's place by the sick child; and Hetty being at liberty wrapped her cloak about her, and went out.

The small captain was lying at death's door; but there were other things to be considered, and Hester Wright's brain was full of a daring project just then.

Mrs. Flannigan was doing very well with Hetty's basket; so she was at liberty to use her own time as she thought fit, and as the old woman would scorn to rob the singer, her pockets were not quite empty. It was the middle of the day - dull and cloudy, a slight drizzling mist falling now and then.

Hester stepped into one of the tramcars, and after a ride of about half-an-hour found herself in a pretty suburb of the great city. She was going to see Sister Mary Vallence, and sincerely hoped that she might find her at home. Her errand was important, and the whole success of the scheme which she was forming in her mind would depend on this young lady's co-operation.

Sister Mary was fairly popular amongst the people for whom she worked. She was a brave, fearless, high-minded girl, never leaving a stone unturned to help others, and influencing many people by the power of a great love. She was at home, and Hetty Wright was at once admitted into her presence. Hetty had never before come in contact with Miss Vallence. Popular as she was in the slums, her rather remarkable face and her great gift of song were both unknown to the young lady. The fact, however, of Hester wearing a poor gown, and one look into her rather worn and pathetic face, ensured her a kindly and interested greeting. Sister Mary asked Hester to seat herself, and then sat quietly down, with that look of leisure on her face which always gives assurance to the teller of a story. Sister Mary did a great deal in her life, but she was never in a hurry; and this fact weighed now with Hester giving her confidence, and causing her heart to beat quietly.

" I ha' come to trouble you with a sad tale, madam,"

L. T. Meade

she began.

"I am sorry - will you call me sister, please," responded the young lady.

"Bet Granger has told me of yer," continued Hester. "You were good to her poor mother."

"Certainly, I had a great regard for Mrs. Granger, - she was good. I know she was difficult to understand, but she was a woman with a great faith. I have often been sorry for her daughter; how is she now?"

"Lost, ma'am - lost, as far as we know - we can't get word nor trace of her. She's not in Liverpool, and I don't know where she be. I fear me she's in the clutches of a bad man, and I ha' come to you to-day, Sister Mary, to ask you to help me to save her. Listen. I can tell in a few words her story, since the night as her mother died."

Hester's great gift was song, but even her speaking voice was refined, pathetic, and with some uncommon notes in it, which always exercised a certain influence over those who listened to her. She told of Bet and Will, of their love and their despair; and the sad tale certainly lost nothing by her manner of telling it. Sister Mary no longer sat still; she rose to her feet, clasping and unclasping her white hands, her lips opening, as if she must arrest the speaker's words - as if she must pour forth some of the pent-up feeling which the story had aroused.

"Then you believe," she said at last, "you firmly believe, that the man, the sailor with the blue eyes, whose face haunts me still, is innocent? - that he never stole my purse - that he is lying in prison now under a false charge? Oh, how glad I am! It seemed to shake my very faith to have to believe that a man with a face like that was really guilty."

"He is innocent, sister. Will Scarlett told a true story. Dent gave him the notes because he wanted to get rid of them, and because he wanted to win Bet for himself. Isaac Dent is the thief, sister; my cousin Will is innocent."

"But if you knew this, Hester Wright - if you were certain on this point," answered Miss Vallence, "why did you not come to the police-court the other day, and clear the sailor? Oh, I think it was cruel of you to stay away."

"What's *my* word, lady? I know it, but I can't prove it. The facts are all agin' Will - he's in the House of Detention now, and he says he's safe to get two year."

"Two years' imprisonment, when another man did the deed!"

"Yes, sister - he says he's quite sure."

"But this is dreadful! I will speak to my father - you must tell your story to my father."

"That'ull do no good, lady. Facts go agin' Will, and there's only one way of clearing him."

"Oh, is there a way? How glad I am! You are a brave girl, Hester. Tell me at once about the way."

"I can't tell you much, Miss Vallence, but I ha' come

L. T. Meade

here to-day - I ha' come to say - yes, to say that we can't never clear Will, and that a plan I have got in my head can't be carried through without you,"

"Without me? Yes; I will certainly help - tell me what I can do."

"I can't lady - not yet-the time ain't ripe yet; but ef you'll trust a lass like me, and give a promise, then I can carry out my plan. And ef it succeeds Will will be cleared, and Bet won't be tied for life to a villain; and a bad man - perhaps two bad men - 'ull meet what they deserve. Oh," continued Hester, "I never said as I believed in God - I never went in for being a good 'un in any sense; but I think I do believe in Him now - I think I do. Trust, and He will bring it to pass. Lady," here Hester resumed her usual manner, "I ha' come to ask you to give me a promise in the dark."

"That is a difficult thing to give," replied Miss Vallence, slowly. "I am most desirous of helping you - I may say further, that I certainly *will* help you to the best of my ability; but a promise in the dark seems scarcely right - why do you ask it of me?"

"Because you can help me in no other way, Miss Vallence. It's just a question of trusting a lass you ha' never seen afore. No harm shall happen to you - not a hair of your head shall be touched, but you must go blindly with me, - in the dark - that's it; there's no other way."

"You're a strange creature" said Miss Vallence. "You move me, you excite me. In spite of myself, I cannot help believing in you. I may be wrong, but for once I will be guided by the queer influence you have over me - by the something within which compels me to trust you. Hester Wright, I will promise to do what you want."

Hester's earnest dark eyes filled with tears.

"You ha' taken a load off me," she said. "There is a good God - for He made you. The lad has a chance now, and Bet has a chance; and perhaps the little 'un may get well arter all. Oh! every thing may come right arter all, and it 'ull be owing to you, just because you weren't afeard, and trusted a lass you had never seen. Miss Vallence, it won't be to-night, nor to-morrow night - but the night arter - some time the night arter - I'll come here, and then I'll ask you to go with me. You needn't be afeard; no one in all Liverpool will be safer nor you; but you'll be coming with me in the dark. A brave lady! Eh! I used to think as ladies had no real sperrit, but I'll never think so no more!"

"I'll be ready for you, Hester," said Sister Mary, in her gravest voice. "The night after next - at what hour will you call for me, Hester?"

"Sister, I may not come at all, and I can't name the hour - it may be any time atween eight o'clock and midnight. I may fail - only I don't think so."

"You will not fail," said Miss Vallence. "I will be ready."

They clasped each other's hands and parted.

CHAPTER XXIX.

If ever a girl ought to feel happy it should be on the eve of her wedding-day. To a great many, however, this turning-point in life, this step into a new and unknown world, is fraught with terror and distress. Wedding bells do not always mean happiness.

Bet Granger was sitting alone in Jenny's attic. She was to be married before the registrar to-morrow to Isaac Dent. He had made all arrangements, and had come over from Liverpool that day to see his promised bride. He had spent half an hour with Bet - had told her when and where to meet him the next morning, and then had gone back to his old haunts, a victorious and satisfied man.

When he left her, Bet had gone up to the attic, and had sat there ever since without moving or speaking. Her hands were clasped loosely in her lap, and her dull and heavy eyes were fixed on the fire. Jenny, finding her poor company, had gone out, and Bet was quite alone. She was to be a bride to-morrow, - Isaac Dent's bride. Her heart beat slowly and calmly; there was nothing more now to hope for; she would keep her promise, and she would try to endure the life which stretched before her. After all, the mate of a sailor had some advantages, - she could often be parted from her lord; he could go away on long voyages, - he could be, he would be, he must be, months away from home; and during that time the very winds that blew, the very breezes that fanned her cheeks, would help to divide them - would help to show her how many miles stretched between her and him.

Yes; the thought of the coming separation, of the certain and inevitable separation, cheered Bet, and made her feel that her lot was endurable.

She was to be a bride to-morrow! How strange! She felt accustomed now to the idea of being almost a bride. It was only a few weeks back that she sat in another attic waiting for the dawn of another wedding-day, and the embrace of another bridegroom. She had not been happy then, - she had been full of fear and apprehension; but the heart now so queer, and dull and heavy, had beat fast, and the eyes had been bright with intense excitement, and in her restless dread and earnest longing she had paced the floor of Mother Bunch's attic until the very dawn. Then she had been unhappy, but she had been alive. Now, what had come over her? Had the spirit of the real Bet Granger gone away with Will over the dancing sea? Had it refused to be parted from her true lover, and was Isaac Dent only marrying a dead woman?

During the fortnight that Bet had spent at Warrington she had searched high and low for her father and the boys. Of course, she had searched in vain. It was quite possible for a clever man like Dent to furnish her with endless clues which all led to nothing. His object was to give her a reason for remaining in Warrington - his object was to keep her at any hazard out of Liverpool. He knew that in Liverpool the knowledge of his treachery towards Will could not long be concealed from her. She would meet Hester Wright - she would meet one friend or another who would certainly tell her that the lad for whom she had sold herself was still in prison.

After they were married - oh! then it mattered nothing at all. Then his triumph would be all the greater when the bad man showed her that, although she was his absolutely, she had done nothing for Will by her deed of self-sacrifice.

Jenny had been a good friend to Bet during the last fortnight. She knew Dent, but did not admire him; and it was an unceasing puzzle to her how any promise could bind Bet to such a man.

"You'll be his forever," she said. "Well, I wouldn't have him - not for no price. I wouldn't be his wife, not if you was to pay me for it. And the other lad, he'll come back from sea, and he won't like to see you Isaac's wife. It's a wrong promise you ha' made, Bet Granger; and you needn't go for to tell me nothing else. If I was you, I wouldn't keep it. Don't 'ee, now, Bet - don't 'ee. Think of the other poor sailor feller - how he'll look at yer when he comes back from sea!"

At first, when Jenny spoke like this, Bet had shut her up with a few sharp words, but of late she had taken no notice; her face every day had grown duller, and her words further apart. Her whole attitude was so dull and lifeless that Jenny gave up teasing her; and finding that, from being an entertaining companion, she was now one of the dullest, left her a good deal to herself.

Bet sat on in the attic, and presently the fire went out, and only the moonlight lit up her little dreary room.

Bet closed her eyes, and fell into a heavy doze; she slept for about ten minutes, and, whether that sleep had refreshed her, and lifted a cloud from her brain, no one can say, but she awoke in quite a different mood: the apathy and indifference of the last few days had left her; she was once more keenly alive, keenly suffering and rebellious.

The events of the two last months - all the story which had come to her since her mother's death-kept flitting like a series of pictures before her vivid imagination. She saw Will's face with a tender light in the eyes; she felt his breath on her cheek, and her hand seemed again to be clasped in his. Once more she heard Hester and Will singing together -

"I had a message to send her-
To be whom my soul loved best,
But I had my task to finish,
And she had gone home to rest."

Bet saw once more the little room in Sparrow Street, and the smile, the look so full of satisfaction, on her dead mother's face.

"Oh, mother, mother!" she sobbed.

She fell on her knees, and the tears streamed through the fingers which covered her face. "Oh mother! life ha' gone hard - bitter, bitter hard - for poor Bet. I ha' broke my word to you - and the lads, I dunno where they are. Oh, I'm good for nought - I'm good for nought - I wish I were lying dead beside my mother!"

She sobbed and sobbed; and her tears, while they seemed to rend her heart, brough a certain sense of

L. T. Meade

lightness and relief.

"Mother, you was a good woman-you believed in religion and all that. I didn't. I were allers a hard 'un - allers, and allers; but I'd give the world, - mother, mother, hear me, hear me, ef you can, up in heaven with God! - I'd give all the wide world to be *good*, GOOD, to-night!"

Again Bet seemed to hear Will and Hester singing to her -

"And I know that at last my message
Has passed through the golden gate,
And my heart is no longer restless,
And I am content to wait."

She rose to her feet. Her tears were over, her great grief was lightened, but now a curious and inexplicable desire took possession of her. She would not fail Isaac Dent. If she had broken every other promise she would at least keep this one. She would marry him tomorrow, and perhaps her mother's God would help her to be a good wife to him. But she would - she must - go to Liverpool tonight. She had money enough in her pocket to take her there; she looked at the coins, going close to the window to see them the better in the moonlight, and saw that she had sufficient to purchase a single third-class fare. How was she to get back to Warrington in the morning? How was she to meet Dent at the registrar's office? She did not know; she felt also that she did not care. Already her marriage with Dent seemed to be removed into a dim and intangible future. She would marry him, - oh, yes - but when and how she did not know, she did not care. She could scarcely bring her thoughts to bear on the great and terrible subject which an hour ago had filled her whole horizon. Liverpool, the great city, was drawing her, as though it was the voice of Will himself. She rose, brushed out her hair, plaited it, and wound it in a great coronet round her beautiful head, washed her face and hands, wrapped her mother's shawl tidily round her, and ran downstairs.

At the door she met Jenny.

"Good-bye, dear," she said in a gentle tone. And she stooped and kissed the little round-faced girl.

"Why, Bet, are you mad?" said Jenny. "Where are you going? How spry you look! And your eyes are so bright! Oh, Bet, Bet! have you come to your senses? Are you going to break your promise to Dent?"

"It is not that," said Bet. "I'll be here tomorrow morn. I won't fail Isaac. I'll see you again to-morrow morning, Jenny, but I must go to Liverpool to-night. My heart draws me - I must go. Good-bye, Jenny - good-bye, dear."

Jenny looked after the tall, stately figure.

"Well, this *is* a rum go," she muttered. "And ef she don't hurry she'll be late. The last train goes at eight o'clock - she'll lose it ef she don't run."

But Bet did not lose the train.

L. T. Meade

CHAPTER XXX.

Isaac Dent did indeed feel himself a triumphant man. If such a nature as his could possibly know anything of love, he had something which he called by that name for the handsome girl whom he had deceived, and whose happiness he had wrecked. His powers of loving, however, might have been described as uncertain, dubious, and absolutely unworthy of so high and sacred a name. But there was no doubt at all with regard to his powers of revenge, or as to his cunning and double dealing.

It was the night before his wedding; and the prize - the choice, rich, great prize of the bravest and most beautiful girl in the city - was almost his. Will was safe in prison; Bet was safe at Warrington. One week of happiness with her, and then he would secure for himself a good berth on board a prosperous ship, and sail away, the luckiest fellow in the land.

If Dent had a conscience at all, it was a very dull one, and it certainly gave him no trouble some qualms that night. He still possessed seven or eight pounds of the stolen money, and he intended to have a right good time with Bet - to spend his ill-gotten wealth freely, and to enjoy himself in a thorough manner for once in his life. He had been to Warrington and made all final arrangements; and now, about nine o'clock in the evening, he left his lodgings to fulfill an appointment he had made with Granger, who was to meet him and was to have a good time with him at the Star and Garter.

Dent's lodgings were close to the docks; and to go from there to Granger's place in Sparrow Street he generally walked up a very narrow and very disreputable street. He could have gone around, going along Castle Street and down by Lime Street; but the other way was a great short cut: and to meet low people, to hear the voices of tipsy men and loud-voiced women gave him no manner of annoyance. At the time of this story there were some courts in Liverpool which at night-time were absolutely in the dark. Not a single ray of gaslight illuminated them. The doers of evil liked such places; and the courts at nightfall were often full, and sounds the reverse of edifying were apt to proceed from them.

David Street, the short cut which Dent was about to take to keep his rendezvous with Granger, possessed several such courts. It was not far from the Irish quarter, where Mother Bunch held undoubted sway. David Street was not quite so much dreaded as Paradise Bow; but, on account of these same dark courts, few respectable people would care to walk there after nightfall. Dent, however, could scarcely be reckoned amongst this class, and he stepped quickly now through the na'rrow street with its flickering gaslight reflecting a sombre glow on the puddles at his feet, and on the faces of the ragged children and men and women who jostled past him. The only bright places were the public-houses, where the hungriest and most despairing paused to look in and long for the brightness and warmth inside. Those who had pence in their pockets generally entered through the swinging doors; those who had not, looked in with growing envy and increasing despair on their faces.

Dent was by no means a sober person, and more than one public-house in David Street knew him well; but he was bound now for the more select Star and Garter, and did not pause before any of the swing-doors. The gas-lamps in David Street were few and far between, and Dent presently came to a part of the street which evidently remained after nightfall in a state bordering on darkness. He planted his foot in a puddle; he nearly slipped on a piece of orange-peel, and found himself swearing under his breath. The next moment, out on the still night air, floated a heavenly sound. It was a woman's voice, singing a rollicking sailor-song. Pure and limpid rose the notes - the air was very taking. There was a chorus to the song, in which many voices joined vigorously. Between the choruses came the single, sweet, captivating voice. Dent stood still. All these sounds came from one of the dark courts. He had a passion for music - he could sing a little himself; he found himself instinctively beating time with his foot, and adjoining in the chorus with his voice. He stood motionless. Instantly one or two other wayfarers did likewise. Dent became the nucleus of a little crowd - each passer-by added to it, all attracted by the voice which rose and fell, accompanied now and then by the rough choruses, but more often singing alone.

The crowd outside began to push towards the entrance of the court, and Dent went with them.

Just inside the court stood a broad-faced, burly-looking woman, holding a lantern in her hand. She flashed its light on each new-comer, and Dent felt dazzled for a moment with the strong glare which was turned upon his face. He thought he heard a chuckle - he was certainly pushed far into the court. The singing ceased, - a voice said: "Now! now, Hetty, - yes, it's all right, Hetty." He turned to go away; but, in what seemed less than an instant, his hands were tied behind him, his mouth gagged, and he was borne aloft in the arms of several people, who began to run with him, he did not know where.

CHAPTER XXXI.

When Bet got to Liverpool she went straight to Paradise Row. She intended to spend the night with Mother Bunch, to borrow a little money from her, and to return to Warrington by an early train in the morning. It was about half-past nine when she reached the Irishwoman's house. There was considerable noise and merriment going on within, and Bet heard the scraping of a fiddle, the air of an Irish jig, and the tap-tap of feet as they danced on the floor. She paused, with a sense of dismay stealing over her. Her nerves were highly-strung - she was in an excited, exalted state, and the loud mirth was particularly uncongenial. She wondered if she could slip upstairs unperceived - she wondered if her old attic were still unoccupied. The door of Mother Bunch's room was wide open - bright light streamed into the passage; but Bet making a dart rushed past the door, and went up the dark, broken, dangerous stairs. She reached the old attic, and then started back with an expression of dismay. It was undoubtedly occupied. A candle burned in a shaded corner; a clean bright little fire shone in the grate; a table, with a cloth on it, held medicine, and a glass; and on the bed where Bet herself used to lie slept a child. She was turning away, with a cold feeling round her heart - she had always fancied, doubtless without any reason, that Mother Bunch would keep the little attic vacant for her. She crouched down on the landing, waiting until the merriment should cease downstairs before she sought Mother Bunch.

Presently she heard the sleeping child stir restlessly, and moan in a very feeble manner. This sound smote on her heart.

"Whoever have the charge of that poor lamb don't set much store by it," she commented. "I'll go in and speak soft to the child. Dear heart, what a feeble moan - it might a'most be a baby."

She took off her heavy shoes, and crept back into the room. The outline of the form in the bed was not that of a very little child.

"About the age of the captain or the general?" murmured Bet. "I must be careful if the young 'un's weak not to startle the poor lamb."

She stirred the fire very gently, and seeing a little sauce-pan with something simmering in it on the hob, tasted it, and found it was beef-tea. She poured a little into a cracked tea-cup, and when the child moaned again - and this moan was even fainter than the last - went up to the bed, determined to act the part of the absent mother, who was so shamefully neglecting her sick child.

"Here, honey, take a sip," she said, and she put her strong firm arm under the restless little head. The small face was in shadow. Bet raised the head higher. "Drink, dearie," she said again. There was a pause. Bet's own face could be seen - Bet's own face could be recognized.

"Bet - Bet!" said the captain - "oh, Bet - I did ax God to bring you back to me!"

CHAPTER XXXII.

When Bet Granger ran past the open doorway of Mother Bunch's room she had very little idea that in a corner of that room, tied firmly into a chair, sat her bridegroom of to-morrow - Isaac Dent.

The gag had been removed from his mouth, but his hands were still firmly pinioned, and he was so securely strapped into the chair which held him that he could scarcely move a limb. Under these circumstances Dent did not show to advantage. There was none of that conscious innocence which gives to other men a certain nobility in the hour of trial. On the contrary, his face was blanched with the most unmistakable fear, and his restless shifting eyes looked no one member of the motley group who surrounded him full in the face.

To all appearance, however, these people did jot take the smallest notice of Dent. They left him in his corner, and eagerly pursued their own gay revelries, deaf to the sound of the piteous voice which he raised now and then. Patrick O'Flaherty, Mother Bunch's husband, played the fiddle with much spirit, but Mother Bunch herself was the real mistress of the ceremonies, footing it bravely in the jig, and letting her voice peal forth in such enthusiastic Irish songs as "The Shamrock," "Garryowen," "Saint Patrick's Day," and the like.

Hester Wright alone stood grave and silent at a little distance from Dent, She was impatient of the mirth, and there was a troubled, anxious look on her face. She did not join in any of the songs, and at last, going up to Mother Bunch, she said a few words in her ear.

" Right you are, child," replied the Irishwoman. "Frinds - we'll now, if you plaze, stop these tokens of mirth and victory, and attend to the business of the evening."

Instantly the fiddle ceased; the footsteps became motionless; the voices died into silence; and a little group of about twenty people formed a semicircle round Dent. Mother Bunch, who was in the centre of this group, stepped forward a pace or two. Her brawny arm was bare to the elbow. She raised it now with a slightly significant gesture.

"Child," she said, addressing the prisoner - for surely as such Dent had to consider himself now - "I ax you a plain question, and I ax it in the name of the frinds of love and order here assembled. Will you confess yourself a guilty man, and own to the maneness of your nature in concocting a plot to ruin the innocent boy, Will Scarlett? or will ye keep your lips shut, and feel the power of this right ahrum?" "You're all a set o' cowards," burst from Dent. "Let me go free, this minute - I'll have the law of you - I had nothing to say to Scarlett's imprisonment."

"Yes, you had, child; and there's no use in your going for to deny it. You stole the notes and the gold, and the purty bit of a purse, and you put the blame on Will, 'cause you wanted to get scot-free yourself, and you wanted to take his gurl from him. You're a bad boy,

Isaac Dent, and you desarves the least taste in life of the rod. Come along, neighbors, hould him, and do your dooty."

Dent began to scream abjectly, and at this juncture Hester Wright stepped to the front.

"Isaac," she said, in her deep, grave voice, "you have got to submit. We plotted this, I and these good Irish friends of mine. I don't mean that Will Scarlett shall lie in prison for your good pleasure. I don't mean that his good lass shall give herself to you. We plotted this, and we means to see it through. You're a bad man. Isaac, and you deceived Bet, and pretended to set Will free, when you know that he lies still in prison. Bet would have married you, I don't know how soon, - perhaps to-morrow - perhaps the next day, - but now she shall never wed you, Isaac; for here you stay - here you stay, year in, year out, until you confesses the truth."

"Yes - here you stay," repeated the Irish voices in full chorus, and the women began to laugh, and the men to chuckle audibly,

"You don't mean it," said Dent. His white face grew several shades more chalky.

"Yes," continued Hester, "we do mean it. You have managed to escape the law, Dent, and you managed to put the best man in Liverpool under its ban. But we've made a law ourselves, and we'll carry it out on you. Here you stays until you confesses the truth about Will. It ain't no good for you to make a fuss, for the police they doesn't often walk down Paradise Row. Mother Bunch is the only policeman as has much power here. You had better submit, Isaac, for you ha' got no loophole to act contrarywise."

"And ef you felt this right ahrum, child, you mightn't like to feel it a second time," burst in Mother Bunch, as she brandished this powerful member in Dent's face.

"What am I to do?" he exclaimed. "I can't stay on here - I - I - just can't. You ha' got me in your power. You'll rue it some day. Er I say what you want me to say, I'll go to prison instead of Will. It ain't in reason to expect a feller to say a thing like that."

"Isaac," continued Hester, "we don't care nothing about punishing you. This is what you've got to do, - you've got to take Will out of prison, and let him marry his own true love. And you have got to do it in this way. I'm going now to fetch Miss Mary Vallence, the young lady whose purse you stole, and she'll take down your full confession in writing, - all about how you planned to ruin Will, all your reasons, and what you did with the rest of the money. She'll put it down on paper - the truth, the whole truth, and nothing but the truth; and then you ha' got to sign your name to it, and Mother Bunch and me we'll witness it, and then after that, Isaac, we'll set you free, and one of us will go with you to the end of Paradise Row, and you shall have an hour - jest one hour - to get away in, before Miss Vallence lodges that paper with the police. Them's our terms, Isaac, and you ha' got to say yes or no to them at once."

"Maybe the child 'ud rather feel my right ahrum," burst from Mother Bunch.

"No," said Isaac, sullenly. "You have me in a trap, and I must do what you wish. You'll be true to your promise about the hour, Hester. Oh! - it's the meanest trick that was ever played on a feller, and I'll be even with every one of you yet."

"You may do your worst, child - we ain't afeard," responded Mother Bunch. "Three cheers, boys all - for Isaac Dent have lost his sweetheart."

The room rang again with the sound of boisterous merriment, and in the midst of the confusion and uproar Hester slipped away.

She was going to Miss Vallence, to ask her to come with her at once, and so to redeem her promise.

CHAPTER XXXIII.

The dread of corporal punishment, the dire sensation of fear, is about the only weapon which produces salutary results on certain individuals. They belong to the lowest of the race, but they undoubtedly do exist, and it is well to know how to deal with them. The Irish people in Paradise Row obtained from Isaac Dent what no amount of prayers and supplications would have won from him. Miss Vallence, when she arrived, took down from his lips a full and free confession of the evil part he had played. This paper was duly signed and attested, and the prisoner was given his liberty and an hour's grace. That he made good use of this hour is apparent; for no one has heard or Been anything of him in Liverpool again. The Irish folks were intensely triumphant; and Mother Bunch, in high good humor, invited every one of the conspirators to a banquet at her house on the day on which Will was let out of prison.

"And now to find Bet, and to see how the little cap'n is getting on," said Hester. "I'll run up and take a look at him now, Mother Bunch. I hope Biddy has not stirred from him during the evening."

"No fear of that, child," responded Mother Bunch, but in reality there was much fear; for the recreant Biddy, Mrs. O'Flaherty's eldest daughter, had been enjoying herself in a back part of the kitchen during the entire evening's entertainment. She slunk away now, afraid to meet her mother's wrath, should it descend upon her devoted head. Hester, accompanied by Miss Vallence, went upstairs.

"It's all very well," she said. "We ha' got rid of Isaac Dent, and poor Will is cleared. But where's Bet! It'll be a sad day for my lad when he gets his liberty, and can't get no tidings of the gel he have given his heart to."

"Oh, we must find her, and we will," said Miss Vallence. "God has helped us - we must not begin to doubt Him now."

Hester stared at her companion.

"I believe in Lord God Almighty," she then said in a solemn tone. "After to-night, I believe in God."

As she said this she stepped into the attic.

"Miss Vallence!" she said, with a glad cry. "Oh, Miss Vallence - come here!"

Hand in hand the two girls approached Bet's humble little bed. A child lay there in a light and refreshing sleep; his head rested on a girl's breast, and her right arm was thrown protectingly over him. The girl, too, slept, and her disordered red-gold hair half covered her face.

In such a manner, therefore, this short history comes to an end. For the captain got well again, and the general was discovered to have found a home for himself in the shelter for children provided by the society for the

L. T. Meade

prevention of cruelty to these defenceless and helpless little beings. Granger thought it best to leave Liverpool, and as soon as possible Will regained his liberty.

Yet again there came the eve of a wedding-day; and on this occasion the day itself dawned brightly and ended in happiness.

These things happened a few years ago, and Bet is a matron now, with golden-haired and beautiful children of her own. She is a grave-looking woman, and in some ways she will carry the sting of that two months' agony to her death. She is religious too; but she says little about her belief, she only acts on it. The sailor Will has the best home in Liverpool, and those who are in trouble have a way of coming to Bet for help and counsel. No one would recognize this sober and yet beautiful sailor's wife for the wild, impetuous, headstrong girl who had vainly made a promise by her mother's death-bed. She has made a promise now, however, which she is not likely to break; and Will says proudly that no one ever had such a wife as his Bet.

Hester was always a Bohemian, and will doubtless remain so to the end. She still sings to the children, and the old people, and the sorrowful. She won't sell her gift; therefore she is likely to remain in so-called poverty for the remainder of her days. In reality, however, she is rich; for a crown of love rests on her brow, and warms her heart.

"I'd rayther," she says now and then, in close confidence, to Bet-"I'd rayther be just what I am-a singer of the slums-than be the greatest lady in the land."

This statement may be difficult to believe, but in Hester's case it is literally true.

L. T. Meade